I0762083

PRAISE FOR *DEATH OF A CHRISTMAS TREE SALESMAN*

"I see Sam Shovel right up there with Frosty and Rudolph —he'll go down in history!" — Kathy Buckmaster

* * *

"Cookies, candy, presents...and murder! A holiday mystery that will leave you questioning...and craving sweets!"
—Niko Sollazzo, @nikosbookreviews, BookTuber

* * *

"A take on Santa Claus that you've never seen! This little mystery will keep you on the edge of your seat!"
—Noelle Austin

* * *

"Patricia Meredith's recipe for a perfect Christmas mystery? Magic with a dash of murder."
—Jess Brady, @jess.literarylife, Bookstagram Reviewer

* * *

"Patricia Meredith never fails to deliver a page-turner with endearing casts, enthralling mysteries, and a slice of life atmosphere. A must-read author!"
—Kayla, @kayshiddenshelf, BookTuber

* * *

"You will love this cozy, Christmas mystery full of charming, quirky characters and numerous Christmas traditions from around the world." —Lydia Pierce

* * *

"The most adorable story! If you love cozy mysteries with big Christmas spirit this is the book for you! Wonderfully written and a joy to read! I definitely recommend!"
—Melissa, @christianbooksandcoffee, Bookstagram Reviewer

* * *

"A definite winner read for anyone looking for that cozy, nostalgic Christmas feel with murder thrown in!"
—Tori Tecken, Author and BookTuber

* * *

"An absolutely charming and unique Christmas story. I really enjoyed the world-building of this particular Christmasland!" —Kirsten, @recipebookworm, Bookstagram Reviewer

* * *

"A wonderful tale filled with Christmas references. This is a new Christmas tradition for us!" —An Erudite Adventure, BookTuber

BOOKS BY PATRICIA MEREDITH

SAM SHOVEL MYSTERIES

Death of a Christmas Tree Salesman

ANNA KATHARINE GREEN MYSTERIES

A Deed of Dreadful Note

THE SPOKANE CLOCK TOWER MYSTERIES

Butcher, Baker, Candlestick Taker

Cupboards All Bared

Crazy Maids in a Row

SHORT STORIES AND POETRY

Happenings: Poems

Murder for a Jar of Red Rum

Death of a Christmas Tree Salesman

Death of a Christmas Tree Salesman

A SAM SHOVEL MYSTERY

Patricia Meredith

Games Afoot, LLC

Cover art by Patricia Meredith

Cover design by Patricia Meredith

First Printing, 2023

This book is dedicated to my children. May the spirit, magic and wonder of Christmas always fill you beyond December 25th, and may the First Gift of Christmas fill your heart, soul, and mind.

"For unto you is born this day in the City of David a Savior, which is Christ the Lord."

In celebration of Clement Clarke Moore (1779-1863),
author of "Account of a Visit from St. Nicholas,"
more commonly known today as
"'Twas the Night Before Christmas,"
which was published 200 years ago in 1823.

Merry Christmas to all!

NORTH POLE CHARACTERS

Dr. Flick — North Pole coroner

Ernst Tannenbaum — father of Otmar Tannenbaum

Franklin — Ernst Tannenbaum's secretary

Grýla — mother of the Icelandic Yule Lads

Kertasníkir — the youngest Icelandic Yule Lad who once stole candles, but is now secretary to O. Tannenbaum

Merry — the Gingerbread Man

Nick Claus — top Santa in the world, head over all the other franchises on earth, married to Nora Claus

Nora Claus — married to Nick Claus

Nuss Knacker — German Nutcracker, owner of the Nutcracker Suites

Otmar Tannenbaum — owner of the largest Christmas tree supplier in the North Pole

Peppa-Patty Cane — co-owner of the candy cane farms, married to Spear O'Mint Cane, and mother of CanDee Cane

Rudolph — lead reindeer for Nick Claus

Sam Shovel — snowman who only comes to life for twelve days a year

Silver Leaf — fairy, works the front desk at the tinsel factory

Sugar Plum — fairy, supplier of tinsel

FEATURED SANTAS

Baba Noël — Egyptian

Babbo Natale — Italian

Ded Moroz — Russian, grandfather to Snegurka

der Weihnachtsmann — German

Father Christmas — British

Papai Noel — Brazilian

Père Noël — French

Sheng Dan Lao Ren — Chinese

Sinterklaas — Dutch

Snegurka — Russian, granddaughter to Ded Moroz

Prologue

I was dead to begin with.

It's not a big deal. It's a snowman's life. A short one, but a full one.

You see, we have exactly twelve days to live each year. Every year, I get to come to life, and I'm lucky enough to come to life at the North Pole at Christmastime.

So, here I was, standing just like I had the previous year, my fedora nestled upon my head, my pipe in my mouth, listening to the old familiar carols play.

I couldn't remember precise details from my past lives, seeing as a snowman's memory is mostly made up of water, which sloshes about quite a bit, even when frozen. But you see, I've got a secret. Inside my old fedora, I've started leaving myself notes, little ones, tracking the years.

Turns out, this isn't the first time I've come to life just in time to solve a mystery...

1

Visions of Sugar Plums

She flew into my office and sat down on the frozen snowbank like it belonged to her, drizzling bits of glitter everywhere she went. It was a good thing my office was outdoors. What a mess.

The soft glow she naturally provided dimmed slightly as her wings stopped their fluttering and she tucked them behind her back. She brushed a black curl from her forehead, pulling down on her short pink skirt as it hugged her thighs like wrapping on a taffy.

"Hiya, Sugar," I said around my corncob pipe. "What can I do for you?"

"The name's Miss Plum, if you don't mind," she said with

a glare as pointed as my carrot nose. "I heard you've decided to solve mysteries during your time here."

I shrugged. "I figured I'd have some fun before I melted away. I've done so before during my past lives, so I don't see the harm in doing the same."

She continued to give me a hard stare before suddenly bobbing her head. "All right, then, I've got one for you."

"Shoot."

"I don't think that would hurt you if I did, but I'd still rather not." She flicked her curl from her forehead again. "The man I've come to tell you about, however, wasn't shot: he was poisoned."

A murder? Had I ever solved a murder mystery before? I supposed there was a first time for everything, and for me, everything was always a first.

"Oh," I said.

Her eyes widened. "O. Tannenbaum! That's right! How did you know?"

I leaned back on my lower-most snowball and considered the fairy, pushing my pipe from one side of my mouth to the other. Was she playing coy with me? There was no possible way O. Tannenbaum had been murdered.

"O. Tannenbaum? Otmar Tannenbaum? The biggest Christmas tree supplier in the North Pole?"

"That's right. I thought you couldn't remember things from your previous lives." Her violet wings fluttered nervously behind her, dropping more glitter onto the already glistening snow.

"Some things are easier to remember than others," I murmured, touching my fedora—wherein lay my secret notebook

—with one branch hand before moving it nonchalantly to scratch an itch that didn't exist. "So Mr. Otmar Tannenbaum is dead."

"As a doornail," Miss Plum assured me.

"Perhaps you'd better start at the beginning."

The fairy nodded, the loose curl falling across her forehead once more, but this time she was too busy gripping her fingers to push it back. "His secretary found him lying in the midst of his Christmas trees this morning, sprawled out like a gingerbread cookie."

"*This* morning?" I glanced at the waxing gibbous moon in the sky, giving great light that I knew would continue both day and night. One of the best parts of coming to life only during the darkest time of the year up here was that I never had to worry about the sun melting me away.

Miss Plum nodded again.

"You came running to me awful quick."

"'Round here things happen fast, even fast asleep."

I couldn't argue with that. "There was no one nearby when Tannenbaum was found?"

She shrugged. "Not that his secretary could see. When Otty didn't respond, a doctor was called. He...he...he said Otty had been dead since the night before."

"'Otty'? You were on a first-name basis with Mr. Tannenbaum?"

The fairy's cinnamon cheeks blushed red as a holly berry, but she didn't elaborate. "The doc said he died of poisoning, though he couldn't be sure what kind or when he'd ingested it until he got him back to the lab."

"He was awful quick to diagnose poisoning there on the spot."

"There were signs..."

"Such as?"

"Perhaps you'd better ask someone else. I'd rather not go into it."

I shifted my pipe again. "All right."

"The point is, the last thing he would have had was his evening cup of eggnog, and he used to to drink his eggnog more on the rummy side."

"Do you think that's what caused his death?"

The fairy shook her head, more glitter sprinkling about her in a shower of sparkles. No wonder snow sparkled, if fairies were constantly dropping the stuff as they flew over it.

"He *used* to drink it that way. I know for a fact he'd given up the booze," she said emphatically. "He was on a medication for his snow allergy that didn't mix well with his annual red rum."

"And red rum spelled backward is murder."

Miss Plum looked at me sideways. "If there was rum in his eggnog, all I can tell you is that Otty didn't put it there. Someone else must have done so, knowing it would interact with his medication, causing his heart to fail moments after."

It seemed quite the jump for the little fairy, but then, jumping was most likely much easier with wings. I bet she didn't fall often, either, unless it was falling in love with Christmas tree salesmen.

I pulled out my pipe. "And you're sure about this? It would make for a rotten twelve days of Christmas if I were to go around accusing folks of murder when there's nothing to it.

I've got better things I could be doing." None that I could think of at the moment, but still.

"Sure as sugar cookies," Miss Plum said with an emphatic nod that bobbed the loose curl.

"Do Nick and Nora know?"

"The Clauses were the first to be told."

I nodded. It was only right. The Clauses were the reason we were all here, after all. They were the top Clauses in the world, head over all the other franchises on earth, and probably those outside of earth as well. They'd been around for as long as I could remember—at least since the first time I decided to record my lives.

"Why come to me, then? I'm sure they have everything well in hand."

"You know Mr. Claus—he's usually got a cookie in one hand and a glass of milk in the other. He told me he'd retired from the mystery business long ago. Suggested I come speak to you if I thought there was something rummy."

"But you don't think there's something rummy."

"No, I think there's something worse than rummy. I think Otty's been murdered."

She fluttered over to me, her glow becoming brighter as her purple wings dropped more glitter. She leaned in to speak directly to my coal-black eyes, so close I could see the shimmer wasn't just part of her wings; her very skin seemed to sparkle like the surface of sugar cubes.

"I think it was Mrs. Cane," she whispered. "She gets so jealous sometimes of how close Otty and I are. Sometimes she acts like she wishes they were as close as the red and white stripes on a candy cane."

"And you?"

Miss Plum twitched her wings and shook her curl back into place. "Otty wasn't twisted like that."

"Uh huh."

"Honest." The fairy raised her left hand and pointed at her chin, then brought it down in a palm against the fist of her right hand. "I swear there was nothing between us but tinsel."

"Sure. 'Tinsel.'" I winked.

Miss Plum shook glitter over the snow. "No, really." She reached into the pocket bag that hung from the belt of her sparkling pink dress and pulled out a wad of the stuff. "Tinsel."

"Tinsel," I repeated, reaching forward to touch the shiny silver ribbons. "Like for trees?"

"Yeah."

I pulled my branch fingers back and some of the tinsel came with them. The fairy reached forward and helped me disentangle myself. I'd barely touched it and yet somehow it had managed to wrap itself around me like barbed wire. As you can probably imagine, I'm less than inclined toward tinsel.

I nodded my thanks. "And how do you know Mrs. Cane wasn't simply helping him with the candy cane side of decor, versus your tinsel?"

The fairy's cheeks brightened again and she shoved the tinsel back in her pocket. "I don't have to explain myself to you. I didn't kill him. I want you to find out who did."

I crunched down on my pipe and considered the matter. It wouldn't do to have murderers in the North Pole. What would the kids think?

"I'll sniff around, see what I can uncover."

"Thanks," said Miss Plum, fluttering close again to plant a kiss on my cheek. She shivered. "You're ice cold," she said with a smile.

"As cold as they make 'em," I said.

2

Candy Canes and Silver Lanes

When you've only got twelve days to live, life takes on a new perspective. The lights on the Christmas trees shine brighter, the blow-up Santas and reindeer in the front yards don't seem as irritating, and the smell of hot cocoa is never too sweet—even if I've never been able to enjoy the taste.

Contrary to what I'd just told Miss Plum, I couldn't help smiling as I took in the happily glowing world around me. The snow was sparkling under the stars, the moon was high and almost round, and the smells and sounds of Christmas were in the air. If I wasn't a snowman, I'd have said I was feeling warm-hearted.

After contemplating the fact that being on the case somehow brought me joy in a way I couldn't explain—and wouldn't want to try to explain to someone like Miss Plum, who'd just lost someone she obviously cared about—I found my small notebook in my fedora where I kept a journal of past life experiences, though the entries were not more than brief highlights.

I knew I'd been coming to life once a year from December 21st to January 1st at least since 1823, but whether I'd done so for centuries prior to that and never recorded them, I didn't know for sure.

I also knew my name—Sam Shovel; where I lived—the North Pole; and that I'd solved a couple mysteries over the years—enough to cause Miss Sugar Plum to come to me when she thought there was something worth investigating.

That was about it. More might come back to me as time passed, but for now, that was enough to be moving on with.

I slid through the snow down the busy streets, saying hello and offering a "Merry Christmas" to the few friends I remembered and everyone I met along the way. I considered heading to the Clauses' workshop first, as a sign of respect, but after stopping an elf to inquire as to their whereabouts, I learned there'd be no chance of speaking with them this day.

"Not today of all days," said the elf, looking down at me from his lofty height.

I've never understood why some folks picture elves as people of shorter stature, saying that their tiny hands make it easier to build all the toys. These people have clearly never met an elf. They would never dirty their hands with menial labor such as building toys. They're much more likely to be found running a company that supplies toys built across the globe. It was this infectious entrepreneurial spirit that led to the global economy of the modern day, as well as a few choice elves living in hiding—or plain sight depending on how you looked at it—in certain countries.

"Don't you know what today is?" the elf asked, straightening his tie covered in little red-nosed reindeer.

"I'm afraid not. I was only born this morning."

"Oh, I'm sorry." The elf tugged on his left pointed ear. "Well, you see, today's the winter solstice."

"So?"

"So...Mr. and Mrs. Claus will be entertaining the other Santas at the annual meeting. Today's the day they compare notes before the final big Christmas rush begins."

This hadn't been in my notebook.

"I see. Thank you," I said succinctly, rolling forward a bit on my snowballs in deference. It always paid to be polite to elves. One never knew what pull they had with the big man himself. "Perhaps you could direct me toward Mr. Tannenbaum's office instead."

The elf nodded and pointed over my shoulder. "Go back to the candy cane farms, turn left at The Gingerbread House, and follow the gumdrop road. You can't miss it. Christmas trees as far as the eye can see." The elf lowered his hand. "But perhaps I can save you the trip. Mr. Tannenbaum is dead. He struck the harp and joined the chorus, as they say."

"I know."

"Oh," said the elf, tugging on his other pointed ear. "Well... Merry Christmas, then!"

"Merry Christmas to you, as well." I turned and began the long slide down the lighted lanes.

The candy cane farm was not so much a farm as fields with rows that stretched back for miles. Silver lanes marked a walking path through, aglow with small white icicle lights interspersed with silver bells that tinkled in the slight wind. The sweet smell of peppermint hit me in a blow so strong if I'd had actual nostrils it might have been unpleasant. As it was, the smell merely washed over me like a wave of freshly baked…well, candy canes.

Each one grew tall and straight, reaching toward the moon in the star-sprinkled Arctic sky. Far off in the distance, I could hear the low rumble of the crooker making its way along the rows, folding the tops down as it cut the stalks and collected them in the back for future purchase.

As the lights of the crooker neared, I realized it wasn't just any old driver in the front, but one so lively and quick I knew in a moment it was Mrs. Cane.

I waved and smiled around my pipe. After a moment, she waved back and slowed down. Once the rumble and roar had died down enough I could hear the soft tinkle of the jingle bells once more, Mrs. Cane hopped down and crossed the final rows to my side.

Her long white hair was pulled back into two braids, a vibrantly dyed red lock running through each to match her product. Despite her hair color, she was no older than forty, and was said to put the "pep" in "peppermint."

"How d'you do, neighbor?" she greeted, pulling her red work gloves off her hands and wiping her forehead with a red-and-white-striped handkerchief she pulled from the pocket of her overalls. Her skin was well-tanned from long days spent out under the sun and moon—depending on the time of year. "Who knew getting rich was such hard work, eh, kid?"

"Is it?" I asked, genuinely curious.

Mrs. Cane nodded. "It is a family business, after all. Spear is on packaging duty today and I'm supposed to be with him while my daughter CanDee was due to be out here runnin' the crooker, but she caught a cold."

"'Tis the season."

"To be jolly and joyous, not to spread germs, I always say." She chortled at her little joke. "It's not so bad. I get to crank the Christmas carols loud enough everyone in the North Pole could hear them if only the crooker weren't so loud." She laughed again. "What brings you to my fields today, snowman? Want to switch out those old branches for some peppermint twists?"

It wasn't such a bad idea, but I had more important questions in mind. I figured since I'd crossed paths with Miss Plum's top suspect, I shouldn't sniff at the opportunity presented to me.

"I'm headed to Mr. Tannenbaum's about a tree, actually."

Mrs. Cane's face darkened. "Oh. Then you haven't heard. I'm afraid Otmar is...no longer with us."

I decided to play the innocent card, pretend I didn't know what she was talking about. Maybe she'd mess up and say more than she meant to. "Took the North Pole Express, did he? Headed to the equator for the winter? Seems a bad time of year for him to do that. I'd think this was prime sales season for him."

"It most certainly is, but what I meant was: he's dead.

Found this morning." She twisted her handkerchief and shoved it into her back pocket.

"That is most unfortunate. Did you know him well?"

Mrs. Cane shrugged and looked toward the green glow of the Christmas tree farm over the horizon. "He provided the green to go with our red, you know. What's Christmas without a Christmas tree hung with candy canes?"

"I heard he was looking at investing in a little more tinsel this year, rather than candy canes."

Mrs. Cane snorted. "Who told you that?"

I kept the image of sparkles and wings to myself.

"Was it that little fairy? She's been all up in Otmar's cocoa. I know you haven't been around for awhile, but that fairy's been sprinkling more than pixie dust over him. Who wants tinsel these days? I mean, seriously. The stuff's a bio-hazard."

"Not a fan of tinsel, Mrs. Cane?"

She snorted again in response. "Listen, the candy cane's been around since the 1600s—it's been a Christmas tradition for longer than the Christmas tree, for heaven's sake. Tinsel's been around since, what, the 1950s?"

"Actually, I believe it's been around since 1610, when the folks of Nuremberg Germany thought it a good idea to hang bits of silver to reflect the candlelight, though it was most popular in the '50s. Wasn't the candy cane invented in 1670?"

Mrs. Cane leaned back and crossed her arms. "How in the silver bells do you know that?"

I scratched my head. "You know...I don't know. It's a funny thing. Ever since I was born this morning, I've been having the strangest sentimental feeling when I hear certain things. I think it's...*memory*."

"I thought snowmen couldn't remember details from their previous lives."

"Me, too..."

"Well, if you remember anything from today, remember this: never trust a fairy."

3

O. Tannenbaum

I tried not to let Mrs. Cane's words bother me as I continued my crunching slide through the snow toward O. Tannenbaum's Christmas Tree Emporium.

Was it just me, or did Mrs. Cane's words have a little more peppermint bark in them than was warranted?

She obviously didn't care for Miss Sugar Plum, and the same went for how the fairy felt for the farmer. There was something between them, and I was betting on the fact that it wasn't tinsel and peppermint.

At The Gingerbread House beside Milky Lake, I turned left and followed the gumdrop road until it came to a dead end where the lights on the path changed from red to green and the air smelled less of sugar and more of pine.

The trees were the kind that didn't seem to mind the snow, forever true in color. The dark green against the white was picture-perfect, and I could see why Tannenbaum's business was known as the top in the industry.

I slid along through the trees, waving to the birds, squirrels, and other animals I passed along the way. Some of them paused as if in response to my wave, but none greeted me back. It's difficult to tell the talking animals from the non-talking here in the North Pole. One never knows whether the creature will sit up on its hind paws and offer you a "Good morning" or a "Merry Christmas" or whether it'll simply scurry off across the snow, leaving tiny footprints in its path.

Of course, the animals wearing clothes are a dead giveaway, but even then, a squirrel wearing a cap and vest was just as likely to tell you to buzz off in an effort to protect his stash of roasted cinnamon nuts.

When I arrived at the great front doors of the emporium, I was greeted by just such a squirrel. In her shimmery green dress, heels, and bow, I assumed she was the doorwoman for the factory.

"Oh, I don't work here," she said with a giggle. "I'm just waiting for my husband to return with a chainsaw. Silly thing —what did he plan to do? Chew through the trunk of the tree like a beaver?"

I gave a polite laugh along with her. "I wonder, would you mind asking at the front desk as to whether I might speak with the secretary of Mr. Tannenbaum? As you can probably imagine, a snowman has a most difficult time going indoors."

"Of course. What name should I give?"

"Sam Shovel." I almost added "P.I." but decided against it at the last minute. I didn't want to spook the secretary, and hoped she'd speak with me more openly if she didn't know I was on the case.

"I'll be back in a minute!" the squirrel squeaked, and bounded inside the doors as I tipped my fedora to her in gratitude.

When she returned, she had a gnome with her. He was a little under three feet in height, with a white beard that stretched to his boots, covering the front of his blue shirt, brown vest, and matching pants. On his head he wore a Santa cap—one of the red and white variety.

"Sam Shovel?" he asked in a low, gruff, gravelly voice, though his evergreen eyes expressed a twinkling humor.

I tipped my fedora again.

The gnome offered his hand. "The name's Kertasníkir. But you can call me Kertas, at least you did last year when we met. I know you might not remember, but we had one of the best Christmas carol bouts this side of the equator."

"We did?" I needed to check my notes.

"Sure thing. You got me with 'Mele Kalikimaka.' Not another Christmas carol in the world with that word in it."

"I'm sure there's a Hawaiian one or two."

"Well, sure, but I don't know it. I'm an Icelander." He tapped the side of his nose. "You're a sly one, Sam Shovel. I'll be keeping my eye on you this week."

"I'd be most grateful for the help. I'm hoping to speak with the secretary of Mr. Tannenbaum."

"I am he."

"*You're* Mr. Tannenbaum's secretary?"

"Have been for over ninety years now. What? Not enough beauty for you?" He fluffed his luxuriant beard.

I moved my pipe from one side of my mouth to the other. "Just not what I expected."

"No one ever expects a Yule Lad. That's what makes it so easy to sneak down south and wreak havoc. I tell you, it never gets old leaving rotten potatoes in bad kids' shoes. Or that time I went with Hurdaskellir and just stomped around slamming doors all night keeping folks awake." He slapped his knee and laughed heartily. "Used to be I had a penchant for candles, but when folks stopped using them as much, I had to find a new occupation. Thus, secretary to Mr. T."

"I see." I glanced toward the squirrel, who was eyeing Kertas like she was thinking of meeting her husband somewhere else, like the farthest end of the candy cane farm. "Perhaps we could take a turn around the trees? I've got a few questions for you."

"Naturally. I suppose you want to know what happened to Mr. T?" Kertas asked, getting right to the point as we began wending our way through the lights and trees.

"If you don't mind."

"Not at all, not at all. As I recall, last year you decided to play detective, too, and seeing as there's been a murder on your very first day, I wasn't surprised to hear you came calling this morning."

We slid toward the crowded trees, past couples with children and couples without children. As we passed the tenth foraging group, I tightened the scarf around my neck and muttered, "It's a wonder there was no one nearby when Mr. Tannenbaum was killed."

"You're telling me," Kertas growled back. "What he was doing at night in that neck of the woods I'll never guess."

"At night? So you know for certain he hadn't come out early this morning? Died on his way *to* work rather than *from* work?"

"The coroner swears he'd been dead far longer than that. Said he must have been killed last night."

I patted my snowy side. "Surely the snow and the cold night air would have preserved him somewhat, making it difficult for the coroner to mark the exact time of death. It does get below -30° F most nights around here, after all."

"You think I hadn't thought of that? I know very well how cold it gets, but as you also know, most folks up here aren't bothered by the cold."

I knew I wasn't, but I was a snowman. How was I to know the other species at the North Pole didn't mind the frigid weather? Though, now that I thought about it, I'd never heard anyone remark on the chill in the air.

"Maybe it's different once we die?" I suggested.

Kertas shrugged. "I'm just repeating what the doc told me."

"Do you know what time he left the office last night?"

"He always headed home after drinking his evening cup of 'nog at ten o'clock sharp, so usually he'd hit the snow around half past."

"Or half till."

"Clock half full sort of snowman, I see. You keep your clock your way and I'll keep mine my way."

"Was there anyone who came to visit him after normal business hours?"

"I suppose you mean that Sugar Plum fairy?" Kertas gave

me a wink. "Not this night, though lately she's been the one to take him his last cup of 'nog."

"Oh?"

"Yeah, she was too busy with Christmas Day nearly upon us. I'm still the one who made the 'nog for him every night, though, and last night I handed it to him myself."

I slid my coal eyes toward the gnome at my side.

"I didn't kill him, if that's what you're thinking," Kertas said. "I gain nothing by his death. Not like I'm set to inherit the whole farm or anything."

I turned my eyes back to the lane of trees again. Kertas made a good point: I needed to find out who benefited from Tannenbaum's death. So far I had a loving mistress and a dedicated secretary on the scene, but neither seemed likely to have reason to kill a man they admired. Someone else must have been there that night.

"Did you leave with Mr. Tannenbaum?"

Kertas shook his head. "I lock up behind him. Last I saw him, he was dashing through the snow toward home."

On and on we made our way through the trees, seeing fewer and fewer groups out here searching for their perfect Christmas tree. I was beginning to get completely turned around, and wondered how the gnome could keep the area straight.

"Kertas, how did you come to find Mr. Tannenbaum? Like you said, it seems you're leading me to the farthest, most isolated corner of the whole farm."

"I found him 'cause I was looking for him. Good thing, too. If I hadn't...some little tike might've happened upon him..."

For someone known for stealing candles from children just

to teach them a lesson, I was surprised by the tenderness with which he said this.

"I've noticed you've not had any problem in referring to Mr. Tannenbaum as 'murdered.' Perhaps it was an accident."

"It was pretty clear when I found him he'd been poisoned. He'd emptied his stomach along the way, so I could tell which direction he'd come from. There was some blood mixed in. Lips and tongue were swollen. I don't mind telling you I fairly quaked at the sight."

That explained why Miss Plum had been reticent to elaborate, though I wondered who'd told her the nasty details. The way she'd talked, it had almost been like she'd seen him herself.

Kertas was shaking his head sadly. "When you work with a man for almost a century, you get to know a fellow. Mr. T was quite the influencer. He was the one who convinced old Prince Albert to include a Christmas tree in the royal festivities in London in the 19th century. Of course, Christmas trees had been a tradition long before then, but they didn't become A Thing until the Victorians made it Popular. Nowadays Christmas trees are used as S-ANTA's delivery point, since every house has got one in one form or another."

"'Santa's delivery point'? I thought Nick Claus preferred chimneys."

"I think Nick still does like the old chimney entrance, but I meant the S-ANTA, as in the Seasonal Antennae."

4

S-ANTA is Coming to Town

I tipped my fedora back on my head and scratched my snow. "I'm confused."

"You know how the Clauses are the head of the Santa franchises across the world?"

"Sure. There's Santas living under different names in every country that celebrates Christmas."

"Right. Sinterklaas, Père Noël, Sheng Dan Lao Ren, Babbo Natale, der Weihnachtsmann..."

"Yes, and they're all convening today for the annual meeting."

Kertas's white eyebrows rose to meet his hat. "How did you know that?"

"Met an elf along the way." I gestured over my shoulder.

"Of course, of course. I couldn't assume I was the first person you'd seek out, intent on a rematch of our Christmas carol battle."

Apparently, I'd definitely missed some notes from last time.

"Anyway," Kertas continued, "about fifty years back, maybe more, the Santas decided what with inflation and gas prices and all, it would be a lot easier if they could deliver things magically."

"Santa delivering presents to every boy and girl in the world in one night and fitting down chimneys—even when there isn't a chimney—wasn't magical enough?"

"Guess not. But you know how magic is just science some folks don't understand yet?"

I nodded.

"Well, that's what this is. The Seasonal Antennae is a way for the Santas to deliver presents without leaving the comfort of their homes."

"With Christmas trees."

"Correct. Mr. T astutely realized that folks don't use chimneys anymore. More people set up trees than have open chimneys, so he took it to the Santas at their annual meeting and presented the idea of the S-ANTA. 'What if,' he said, 'you could send a signal to every Christmas tree in your region that would physically fax your present of choice under the tree without ever sliding down another chimney?' You can imagine the response."

I whistled.

"Exactly."

"What about the stockings? Santa's got thousands if not millions of stockings to fill on Christmas day."

"As long as they're hung within a ten-foot radius of the tree, the S-ANTA can fill those stockings, too."

"Wow. Santa himself won't be necessary before long."

"Strange as it is to believe, the world existed for a long time before Saint Nicholas. It's only been about five hundred years since he first made his way into European culture, and he's still not celebrated in every country in the world."

"Perhaps it's simply because we live at the North Pole, but sometimes it's still difficult to imagine a world without a Santa Claus."

"Even for a snowman who only lives for twelve days a year."

I nodded. "What a time to live. This is the high point of the Christmas season."

"And yet you've chosen to stick your carrot nose into solving a murder mystery?"

"What else am I going to do?"

"Oh, I don't know: sing Christmas carols, hide a pickle in a couple Christmas trees, decorate a Star of Bethlehem lantern, weave a Yule Goat, build one of those German Christmas pyramids with the little propellers. I used to love stealing all the candles from one of those things and replacing them with stubs." He chuckled at the memory.

I could almost smell the gingerbread and hear the Yuletide carols being sung, the choruses of endless "Glo-o-o-o-o-ria" echoing in my mind.

It wouldn't be that easy to dissuade me, however. I could feel it deep in my snow that I was meant to solve this mystery.

"As Mr. Tannenbaum's secretary, don't you want me to find out who murdered him?"

Kertas grunted and ran a hand through his beard. "Of course I do. I merely wondered why you felt it was *your* job to solve this mystery, rather than someone else's."

"Like who?"

"I don't know. Krampus, maybe?"

The sound of crunching footsteps in the snow gave me a shiver down my back, until I realized it was just Kertas's booted feet making the sound.

"The guy's been itching to redeem his name for centuries," Kertas continued. "He can't help it he's a scary-looking creature."

I tried to agree, seeing as I'd never actually met the guy—at least, definitely not in this lifetime—though his name alone was triggering something in my memories from long ago. "You know what they say: every horrific creature has a mom somewhere who thinks he's the cutest thing in the world."

"Our mother never said that about us Yule Lads. But then, raising thirteen boys couldn't have been easy. Probably why we all turned out the way we did."

"So you'd see Krampus as the *solver* of the mystery, not as the *murderer*?" I asked.

"If you've ever met Krampus, you'd know in a heartbeat he didn't do it. For one, he'd rather beat you at a game of pick-up-sticks, and two, he wouldn't use poison."

"Why is everyone so convinced Tannenbaum was poisoned?"

"I've brought him a cup of 'nog every day for the past ninety years. Two parts eggnog, one part rum. Only, Mr. T stopped taking the rum part about a year ago when they finally diagnosed his snow allergy."

"Miss Plum mentioned something about that," I said. The sound of snow falling off a branch nearby with a *crunch* seemed apropos to our conversation. "How did he survive up here?"

Kertas shook his head. "Poor man. It was starting to look like he might have to sell the factory and move to New Zealand. He'd mentioned more than once the idea of getting into the pōhutukawa tree business instead of evergreens."

"Surely there was a medication..."

Kertas shrugged. "The docs were trying lots of different things, that's why he gave up the rum. Or at least tried to."

"What makes you so sure he hadn't simply decided it wasn't worth the effort and put a couple slugs of rum in his eggnog? Maybe the rum didn't mix well with the meds and—"

"He wouldn't do that. He was meticulous. Wouldn't eat or drink anything fermented even, just in case it was contraindicated. The man was on a strict diet of milk and cookies, just like Nick Claus."

"That can't be healthy."

The gnome shrugged again. "Nick's been doing it for centuries."

"True. So where did the eggnog fit in?"

"It was his one delicacy every evening. Helped him slow down and mull over the day, y'know, like chamomile tea for humans."

"Wait, I thought Tannenbaum was human?"

"Yeah, sure he was, the way the Clauses are human and yet have managed to survive for hundreds of years. Not quite sure what they are, but I don't like to go about asking a person's species—it's not respectful."

I could understand that. "So did you have last night's eggnog tested?"

"Nope. I'd already cleaned the mug last night before leaving. You don't want to leave a mug lying around with a bit of 'nog inside—trust me. The smell alone..." He shivered.

"I don't get it. Why are you and Miss Plum so sure there was something in the eggnog that killed him? Couldn't it have been something else?"

Kertas shrugged. "It's the last thing he had."

"Was there any reason someone might want to kill Tannenbaum? A rival perhaps?"

"Like who? Up here, he's the end all be all. Every year he provided the tree for the Grand Hotel, the one in the park, as well as the Clauses' own tree."

"So sales were good?"

Kertas mumbled something, then cleared his throat. "Well...they've changed, let's say. Even with brilliant advertising techniques like including that whole scene in *A Charlie Brown Christmas* where he dismisses the fake trees and ends up with a real one, more and more people were purchasing fake trees."

"So why doesn't he switch industries? Start producing fake trees instead of real ones?"

Kertas sniffed. "Why do you think fake trees have been more popular lately?"

I adjusted my scarf around my neck, then suddenly understood. "Oh I get it: the S-ANTA?"

"Bingo. The S-ANTA was the answer to two problems at once. It saved Mr. T's Christmas tree industry with a simple redesign, while also allowing the Santas around the world to enter the twenty-first century in their present delivery."

"So it wasn't a rival that came up with the fake trees, it was Tannenbaum himself?"

The gnome nodded and threw a thumb over his shoulder. "If you were to walk the same distance we've come in the opposite direction from the main offices, you would have found fake trees instead of real ones stretching just as far."

"Tannenbaum must be living the tree dream with two successful enterprises."

"He does pretty well for himself. He's the world's top supplier of fake and real trees for the holidays."

"World's top—ha, I get it," I said, laying a finger aside of my nose. "'Cause this is the North Pole—"

Just then, something pelted me from behind, knocking me flat into the snow, and the world went dark.

5

Oh, Holy Night

"Did you see that?" a muffled voice asked above me. "Shovel! Sam! Are you hurt?"

I felt two hands try to lift me up out of the snow. The trouble with being made of snow and then falling into snow is that it's difficult to tell where I end and the fresh snow begins.

After dusting myself off with Kertas's help, gathering my lost fedora and notebook, and unearthing my corncob pipe, I took a deep, cold breath and steadied myself.

"What happened?" I asked.

"That snowball came out of nowhere." Kertas pointed to a lump in the snow where I'd lain. "Went right through you."

I glanced down and sure enough, I could see a hole through

the middle of my lowest snowball. "Brings new meaning to 'hole-y night,' doesn't it?" I chuckled.

Kertas shook his head. "Look at you. And here I thought you'd lost your sense of humor."

"I didn't lose it, I don't think. But it's difficult to know who I am sometimes." I scratched around the hole in my belly. "Do I seem very different from the last time I was alive?"

Kertas shrugged. "Like you said, it's difficult to remember someone you only knew for a few days one year. But I think we're all like that—not just snowmen."

The lump of snow that had impaled me lay there like an ill omen, red as strawberries around the edges, an odd thing to see against the white snow.

"Wait a minute—are you bleeding?" Kertas looked from the red to me and back again. "I thought snowmen couldn't get hurt."

I glanced down at my belly and back at the lump of red-lined snow. I gulped. "I thought so, too."

"Guess that's just the Invincible Snowman," said Kertas, concern filling his eyes as he looked at me in a different light.

"I thought he was the Indomitable or Abominable." I tried to recall and then realized again what I was doing. I was remembering. Maybe snowmen could remember more than I thought, after all?

"Doesn't he wish. More like the Indefatigable Snowman—the guy doesn't let you get a word in edgewise." Kertas leaned forward. "Wait, wait, wait, hold my eggnog." He winced. "Maybe that's not the best turn of phrase at the moment..." Kertas reached out and dusted off the lump that had sailed through me. "It's not just a snowball. It's a brick. Gingerbread buttons! Someone's got it out for you, Shovel, and you're not even a day old!"

"Means I must be on to something," I muttered, taking the brick from Kertas. We both turned around and tried to pierce through the evergreen trees surrounding us with our eyes, but it was no use. "I can't see through the forest for the trees."

"I don't think that's exactly how that saying goes," said Kertas, "but I get your meaning. It must have scared the murderer that I'm bringing you back where I found the body."

I reached forward and packed snow into my missing region. Good thing snowmen are easy to patch up.

"Is this the place?"

Kertas nodded as he looked around. "I think so. When you've worked a place for almost a hundred years, you get to know a thing or two. It smells like the right place."

"Smells?"

"Take a sniff."

I closed my eyes and did as he asked. "Cold, fresh air, clean snow, pine trees, sap..." I opened my eyes. "Peppermint!"

Kertas nodded again and pointed off to the east. "We're close enough to the Canes' peppermint farm on this edge of the forest to smell it on the wind."

"Close enough to suspect they might have had a hand in Tannenbaum's death?"

The gnome peered off into the distance. "Maybe."

"Did you see anyone or hear anything when that brick came flying? Perhaps someone snuck out of the candy cane field?"

"Not a thing. Sorry."

I straightened my scarf and the large wooden buttons on

my second snowball. "Someone must have followed us, or been watching this location to be sure we didn't find any clues."

Taking in the mussed up ground, I knew there was no chance of finding tracks in this mess. "Did you notice any tracks in the snow when you found Tannenbaum this morning? Since this isn't the busiest part of the Christmas tree farm, I'd assume there weren't many to mix up."

I pointed to two long divots through the snow between a row of trees, and the hoof prints alongside them. "In fact, are you even sure he died here? Perhaps someone killed him elsewhere and simply dragged his body here to be found?"

Kertas followed my pointing branch finger. "I think those were made by the coroner's one-horse open sleigh. All the same, you make a good point. Even though I watched Mr. T take off toward home, that doesn't mean he didn't go somewhere to be murdered on the way."

The gnome had a very succinct way of putting things. Since we were near the Canes' farm, perhaps Tannenbaum had been on his way there when his sudden attack hit him and he'd fallen over dead.

Or perhaps Tannenbaum had been on his way to meet Miss Plum here for a rendezvous, since she hadn't made it to his office, and she'd bopped him on the head like Little Bunny Foo-Foo—though she hadn't made it this far north last time I'd been alive. It was possible the coroner had missed a mark like that amidst the clear signs of poisoning.

"Why would someone be afraid we'd find anything here?" Kertas looked around at the snow. "I'm honestly glad to see they cleaned up a bit. It was a mess earlier. But that means there was no chance of us finding any more clues. And you of all people know how quickly snow can cover up a multitude of sins. Who have you talked to, other than me?"

I hesitated. Could I trust Kertas? He seemed like a nice enough gnome, so long as I kept him away from candlesticks, and we'd supposedly been friends last time I'd lived. I was going to need someone's help on this case, might as well be him.

"Not many people. Met an elf along the way, like I said—never did catch his name. Other than him, really just two so far: Miss Plum and Mrs. Cane."

Kertas snorted. "Bet they each pointed fingers at the other?"

"You got it," I said, pointing at the gnome with my pipe.

"Mrs. Cane didn't tell you how much trouble her little candy cane empire is in, now, did she?"

"Well..."

"Candy canes never get old. People reuse them. The candy cane has been around since the 1600s, and yet there always seems to be more. Why? Because they can't give up the family farm."

"Sounds similar to Mr. Tannenbaum's predicament, then."

"True, only she didn't have a way of reinventing her industry like Mr. T did with the fake trees."

A business on the edge of destruction—and I bet tinsel was struggling, too. Was there anything in the North Pole going as well as expected by the little boys and girls down south?

"You don't think one of them could have thrown that brick at me? Do you?" Both women had seemed so genuine.

Kertas didn't answer. He pulled on his beard while I worried on my pipe.

"This is a very interesting situation. A snowman doesn't get in a situation like this every day."

Kertas pulled off his hat, scratched a head as bald as a used candle, then replaced his cap like a candle-snuffer, pulling it snugly down over his ears. "I think I'd better come with you."

"I'd prefer to work independently."

"Then let's be independent together," said Kertas with a wink. "I'll call the doc who picked up Mr. T's body and find out if he's been able to identify the cause of death."

I nodded and let him walk off a discreet distance behind some trees before removing my fedora and pulling out my notebook, opening to my last life.

Mrs. Claus reported candlesticks have gone missing. Asked me to look into it.

Talked with reindeer. Pointed to Gingerbread Man.

GM pointed to Abominable Snowman.

AS pointed to nutcracker factory.

Nutcrackers pointed to Tannenbaum's Christmas Tree Emporium.

Solved.

I smiled to myself. Most likely I'd tracked the missing candlesticks to Kertas, and we'd ended up going out for some pumpkin pie which inevitably led to some caroling. Must've been a good way to end my time here on earth.

I resolved to take better notes this time around, however. After jotting down what I could from my full morning, I went looking for Kertas.

"You gotta be kidding me.... What's this guy doing? Making a list and checking it twice?... Uh huh.... I agree.... I'll be sure to tell Shovel... Uh huh, see you soon." Kertas hit the button on his phone and turned to me. "You're not gonna believe this."

"What?"

"It was poisoning for sure. And what's more, Mr. T died the same way his father did."

6

Cold That Was So Deep

"It-it-it was," the coroner stuttered, "soap poisoning!"

"Soap poisoning? How does someone die of soap poisoning?" I asked.

"If it's m-m-made from a refined amount of mistletoe it can be d-d-deadly if ingested."

Dr. Flick's large frame and glasses were typical of a doctor in my limited experience, but the fact that he was also a moose sometimes surprised people.

"*Viscum album*—European m-m-mistletoe—is quite toxic, though its American cousin *Phoradendron serotinum* is less so. It would appear s-s-someone boiled down quite a collection of mistletoe berries and leaves into a concentrate, then b-b-baked it into soap. It would have only been a matter of a few hours before T-t-tannenbaum began to experience symptoms."

"Like what?" I asked.

"Gastrointestinal distress, d-d-delirium, slowed heart rate, vomiting, diarrhea, swelling of the throat, l-l-lips, and tongue. We can see evidence of all these in his b-b-body." Dr. Flick waved an antler in the direction of the remains of Mr. Tannenbaum.

The morgue's regulated, deeply cold temperature had allowed me to actually view the body. Living in the North Pole had made me less surprised by talking animals, toys that played themselves, trees that sang as they decorated other trees, and magic in general, but there was nothing magical about the blue swollen lips of Mr. Tannenbaum. Just one look had given me a sick, churning feeling deep in my snow, and I'd suddenly felt warm under my scarf.

"But...it must take a lot to kill someone," I said. "What was Tannenbaum doing eating a bar of mistletoe soap?"

"He might not have noticed if it was mixed into his 'nog," Kertas said.

Again with his eggnog theory. If I wasn't careful, I'd be sucked into his way of thinking, rather than keeping an open mind.

"I've never tasted eggnog," I said, "but I'd think the mistletoe soap would be quite bitter."

"Remember, he was used to drinking it with rum. He probably thought I was trying out a new rum-flavored additive and drank it right down." Kertas shook his head. "Silly man. Didn't he know I would've told him if that were the case?"

"Was there anything else in his belly?" I asked Dr. Flick.

The coroner nodded. "Your t-t-typical Christmas treat ingredients: flour, sugar, butter, chocolate, nuts, and a wide variety of spices from cinnamon to c-c-cardamom."

"And what was this about it being the same way his father died?" I asked Dr. Flick. "That must have been many centuries ago. How could you possibly remember?"

"As c-c-coroner of the North Pole, as you can probably imagine, I have l-l-limited work sent my way, so it's easy to r-r-remember past experiences. We generally have the hap-hap-happiest Christmas this side of the world." The moose glanced toward the covered body of Mr. Tannenbaum. "It also only happened t-t-two years ago."

I raised my twig eyebrows and removed my pipe in surprise. I'd missed that in my notes. Why hadn't I been notified? Had they caught the culprit before I arrived on the scene?

"Two years ago this man's father was also murdered by mistletoe? What are the chances?"

"P-p-precisely," stuttered the moose.

"I'd forgotten that," said Kertas.

"How could you forget?" I turned on the gnome. "That should've been the first thing that leapt to your mind when you thought of poison."

Kertas shrugged. "Slipped my mind, is all. In case you hadn't noticed, Christmas time is here. Santa's not the only one who gets a bit busy this time of year."

"I take it Nick and Nora must have caught the murderer?"

"N-n-nope," said the moose, while Kertas shook his head. "No one did."

I removed my pipe and pointed it at my chest for emphasis.

"Was I involved? Did someone ask me for help and I've just forgotten?"

Dr. Flick and Kertas exchanged a look.

"N-n-not that I recall."

"Was his father a fan of rummy eggnog, too?" I asked them, but they both shrugged.

"All I know is, his father—Ernst Tannenbaum—had just come back from a trip along the Milky Way. He seemed over the moon—not literally, of course," said Kertas. "The last thing he said to his son was that he'd see him in the morning, that he'd tell him all the details then, but that another crisis had been averted."

"What crisis?"

"Mr. T—Otmar—never found out. His father was dead by morning." Kertas removed his cap and placed it over his heart.

Of course he was. That was how it always went. Hadn't the man read any murder mysteries? Then again: had I?

"Mr. T still hasn't—or hadn't—gotten over the shock. He always swore he'd solve his father's murder if it was the last thing he—" Kertas looked up in surprise. "Well, cut me to the candle quick. He kept muttering that he'd finally solved it."

"He, O. Tannenbaum?"

"Yeah. Last night." Kertas placed his hat back on his bald head. "He wouldn't tell me what he'd solved. Said he'd tell me in the morning."

The coroner shook his heavily antlered head. "D-d-didn't he learn anything from his f-f-father's death?"

"Why would he, or any one of us, think he'd die?" Kertas asked. "This is the North Pole—the land of good cheer and singing loud for all to hear and good ol' Santa Claus!"

"You think O. Tannenbaum solved his father's murder and that's what got him killed?" I clarified.

"Sure." Kertas snapped his fingers so loudly the sound echoed in the cold room. "*That's* why he was so interested in the pōhutukawa."

"I thought you said it was because he was considering moving to New Zealand."

"I thought so, too. But maybe there's more to it. The legend of the pōhutukawa is that Tawhaki, a Maori warrior, went to heaven to avenge his father's death. That never ends well, of course, and as he fell from heaven, his blood became the bright red flowers of the pōhutukawa."

A sad story for a Christmas tree, I thought. But more than that, it meant it was really *Ernst* Tannenbaum's murder we had to solve.

"Do you know what his father was doing traveling the edge of the galaxy?" I asked. "What he might have figured out?"

"The edge of the—oh, you mean the Milky Way? I take it you don't remember what the Milky Way is?" Kertas asked in return.

I started to reach for my notebook, but then decided I didn't want to reveal I had it in front of Kertas or the coroner. "It's on the tip of my tongue. Somewhere in this snow I remember."

"It's a long story, but I'll try to explain as quickly as possible," the gnome said. "The Milky Way is the first trail the original Saint Nicholas took when he began delivering presents world-wide. Back when he first started, it was a simple matter, but now there are so many kids in the world, the business has had to allow for franchises to cover the multitude of countries. It's caused a wide variety of traditions and Santas to sprout up."

“Thus the council of Santas meeting today,” I said.

“Right. Nick and Nora Claus are the head of the Santa Claus outfit, so they call a meeting every year on the winter solstice. Not every Santa shows up, of course, but they’re required to attend at least five meetings every decade. Keeps everyone connected, I suppose. Makes sure they’re all on the same page.”

“Makes sense. How many Santas are there?”

Kertas whistled. “I’ve lost count. You, Dr. Flick?”

The moose shook his giant head. “At l-l-least fifty.”

“I was gonna say more like a hundred. The more connected the world gets, the more certain traditions get passed around and revamped for that particular country.”

“Like the Christmas tree.”

“Bingo.” The gnome touched the tip of his reddish nose.

“There’s at least one Santa on every continent?”

The gnome nodded. “Even Antarctica.”

“Impressive. That’s quite the empire.”

“Greater than the British, Mongol, or Russian empires ever stretched for sure.”

“Is Nick Claus descended from the original Saint Nicholas then?”

Kertas shook his head. “Nope, but Nora is. Her family’s been keeping the business going for centuries. It just happens that the man she married was named Nick. If the nose blinks, as they say.”

“If the nose blinks?”

“‘If the nose blinks, it’s probably Rudolph.’ Haven’t heard that one yet today?”

“Guess not.” I shrugged and crunched on my pipe. “So,

Ernst Tannenbaum never mentioned anything to you after his trip?"

"No, why would he?" Kertas asked.

"I just figured as his secretary..."

"Oh no, I wasn't Ernst Tannenbaum's secretary, just Otmar's. The original Mr. T's secretary is a turkey."

7

A Turkey and Some Mistletoe

I'd assumed what Kertas meant was that Father Tannenbaum's secretary was no good at his job.

I should have known better.

"It all began back in 1986 when I was invited to Christmas dinner. I thought I was the guest of honor, so I got myself dressed up." The turkey, Franklin, cleared his throat, his tail coverts shaking behind him. "Turned out I hadn't understood the invitation correctly. Thankfully, Ernst Tannenbaum was at the dinner—and a vegetarian—so he invited me to come to his house to stay with him. Got me a job as his secretary and before I knew it, I was set for life."

And Kertas had said the Abominable Snowman was a chatterbox. This particular turkey was a regular "strutting tom."

"But that still doesn't answer my question."

"What was your question, again?"

"Why did Ernst Tannenbaum travel the Milky Way two years ago?"

"Oh, right." Franklin tapped his head with a wingtip. "Old age'll get you every time. Not thinkin' as clearly as I used to. Once upon a time, I was sharp as Santa's whip, I tell you, sharp as a reindeer's antlers, sharp as the scissors used to make ribbon curls, sharp as—"

"Er, yes, so regarding Mr. Tannenbaum?" Kertas interrupted.

"Mr. T—I'm sorry to be the one to tell you, but he died recently."

The turkey was clearly as short on memory as Uncle Billy in *It's a Wonderful Life*.

"That's right, his son died of the same thing his father died from two years ago," I said. "We've just come from Dr. Flick's office, where he told us both Tannenbaums died of mistletoe soap poisoning."

"Flick? Flick who?"

"*Doctor* Flick, the coroner?" I said. "Dr. Flick said he'd just come back from a trip down the Milky Way and we wondered if you might remember anything he said regarding the experience?"

"Dr. Flick took a trip down the Milky Way? Sounds lovely, but why would I know anything about his trip?"

Kertas sighed so heavily it sounded more like a growl. "No, Dr. Flick didn't go, Ernst Tannenbaum did. Two years ago. Before he died."

"Oh, of course, yes, yes, he did. Quite a long trip it was, too. He went all around the world, checking on the installation of the S-ANTA. Have you heard of the S-ANTA?"

"Yes," Kertas and I said in unison.

Franklin nodded, his snood waggling when he did so. "It's a brilliant system, isn't it? Good thing the Tannenbaums invented it. They helped save Christmas, you know? Not a fan of plastic trees myself. They look like they're made from green pipe cleaners. Not sure they really bring Christmas close to a person, if you know what I mean. But to each his own. They've certainly become popular these days. Suppose it's better than stealing a squirrel's home and lighting candles on a fire hazard. The boss always knew what was best, and with the fake trees it was much easier to craft the S-ANTA and get it secretly installed in each person's home. Without that system, the Santas were starting to think it might be time to hang up the red cloak and boots for good. There's just too many children in the world, even with the franchise model."

"Seems more and more parents are spreading the lie of Santa's fakery, too," said Kertas with a shake of his head. "Though I suppose that might make it a little bit simpler of a transition for the wee tikes, should the Santas ever have to retire for good."

"Santa fake?" asked Franklin.

"Yeah," I said. "A lot of parents say they're the ones that fill the stockings, rather than Santa."

The turkey gave an irritated rustle of feathers. "What about the *kahk* and mince pies and *pepernoot* and apples and other treats left out for Santa? Do they say the parents eat those, too?"

Kertas nodded. "What's odd is how many of them truly seem to believe it, or not believe it, as it were. They really don't seem to realize there are extra presents and things in the stockings that they didn't put there."

"Each person probably thinks another family member put it there," I suggested.

"Exactly," said Kertas. "It's sad to think of some kids growing up without a Santa Claus, but some kids have the gift of gifting naturally. We've heard of kids who started playing the role from an early age—as young as six—putting things in their parents' or other family members' stockings because their love language was gifts."

"It's the gift that keeps on giving." I smiled.

Franklin gobbled to himself worriedly. "I suppose it's a good thing I got out of the business when I did. Not that I had much say in the matter, mind you, seeing as my boss was murdered and all. Did you know that Ernst Tannenbaum was murdered just two years ago? And now his son has met the same fate."

Kertas and I exchanged a look. Perhaps we'd best quit while we were ahead. I had a feeling we weren't going to have any luck pulling any useful information out of this birdbrain.

"Murdered by mistletoe—a terrible way to go, so I hear," he gobbled on. "Quite the nasty ingredient. There's a reason why you don't see that stuff hanging around where everyone can see."

"Except at Christmas..." Kertas muttered. "When you see it hanging everywhere..."

"Sure, sure. What I mean is, it's dangerous stuff, you know. Why, did you know Mr. Tannenbaum died of mistletoe?"

"I heard it was mistletoe soap in his eggnog," I said.

"No, he accidentally put mistletoe in his tea with his evening Christmas cookie. You can't go around drinking brewed mistletoe. That stuff'll kill you."

"So I hear," I said, exchanging looks with Kertas. "Did you make him his tea?"

"No, he was at home. I only made his tea when he was at the office. He was a big fan of natural remedies: echinacea, marshmallow root, chamomile, peppermint. He had a book that told him mistletoe could be taken medicinally to treat arthritis, rheumatism, headaches, even cancer, so he probably thought he'd try it in his tea."

"This book didn't warn him *not* to put it in his tea?"

The turkey scratched his head with a wing. "I don't recall. I've got it around here somewhere. Give me a minute."

Franklin wandered back inside, leaving us standing outside his front door to avoid any melting fiascos on my part.

"Should we believe anything this bird says?" I asked Kertas. "The coroner said Ernst died of mistletoe soap poisoning, just like his son, didn't he?"

Kertas nodded. "That's what I took him to mean. But maybe he just meant they'd both died of mistlet—"

"Ouch!" Franklin yelled inside.

"Maybe I should go help him..." Kertas rolled his eyes, then joined the mayhem of noise coming from inside Franklin's abode.

After a great deal of "Now where is that" and the sound of falling books, I finally heard, "Aha! You found it!"

When they reappeared, Kertas had his Santa hat off and was rubbing his bald head where a lump was already forming. Franklin was carrying an unwieldy tome with *Nipping At Your Nose: Natural Remedies for All Your North Pole Needs by Jack Frost, MD* printed in gold lettering down the side.

"Here's the book you asked for." The turkey handed it to me and it immediately fell to the ground with a *whump*, taking my branch hands with it.

"Seven swans a-swimming!" Kertas yelled, thrusting his hat back over his ears. "The man's got twigs for arms! Literally! You can't just go throwing a book at him." He reached down, picked up each of my branches, and none-too-tenderly shoved them back into my sides. "You okay, there, Shovel?"

I nodded.

"Sorry," Franklin gobbled sheepishly. "Perhaps I can look it up for you." He reached down and picked up the book. His wings were certainly stronger than they looked. "Now, what did you want to know again?"

"Just let me do it," Kertas said gruffly, clearly at the end of his patience.

He flipped the book open to the back index, riffled a few pages, then ran his finger down a particular page until he came to what he wanted. Then he flipped to about midway through the book and searched the page with his eyes. "Here we go," he grumbled, holding out the book so I could see.

The information was everything we'd already heard from Dr. Flick and Franklin, but I also tapped the line where it said, "Although death by poisoning is rare, if the European variety of mistletoe is brewed to a concentrated form, it would be highly poisonous and could cause death."

"So why would he do it?" I muttered to Kertas. "It couldn't have been an accident."

"Someone must have mixed it into his normal morning tea without his knowledge," the gnome murmured in return.

I nodded. "Thank you," I said to Franklin as Kertas handed the book back.

"Find what you were looking for?"

"In a way."

"Mr. Tannenbaum used that book often for brewing his medicinal teas. He most likely used it the morning he died, you know. He'd just come back from a trip the night before; he was so excited. Kept saying Christmas had been saved once more. I asked him what the gladsome tidings might be which inspired such happiness..."

Kertas and I leaned in closer.

"But he refused to tell me. Jokingly said if he told me I'd have to be Christmas dinner." The turkey chortled. "I will say one thing, though: it seemed odd to me that he'd be murdered just after he saved Christmas. A maudlin ending to the tale, you might say. Not many Christmas movies I can think of ending that way..."

"He must have been killed because of something that happened on that trip," I said.

"Or who he met on that trip," said Kertas.

"Or...who went *with* him on that trip."

"Nick Claus went with him," Franklin popped in.

I turned slowly to the turkey. "Santa Claus himself? The big man? The head honcho?"

"Of course. He generally made the trek with Tannenbaum once a year, ever since installing the S-ANTA, to be sure everything was in working order. Now that I think about it, he was quite grumpy when they returned. I just assumed it was because Mrs. Claus had switched to skim milk, but maybe it wasn't."

"Tannenbaum was excited and happy...but Nick Claus was grumpy and upset...," Kertas repeated.

My coal eyes practically bugged out of my head. "You're not suggesting—"

"Of course not," the secretary gobbled, shaking his wattle emphatically, but clearly understanding where my thoughts were headed. "No one is saying that Santa murdered anybody."

8

Santa's Big Scene

"All right, now, now listen up!"

The circle of Santas quieted slowly.

"That's better. Now, we've got to come to a decision or we'll be here till Christmas Eve!"

"Noel," someone called out in a deep voice as old as Jack Frost himself.

A snort came from one of the Santas who had fallen asleep, his bundle of furs hiding his face and hands so that he looked more like the Easter Bunny than a person.

"That's the first 'Noel' someone's called out all day," someone else joked.

"Yeah, but Ded Moroz is no angel!"

The circle was suddenly full of jiggling bowls full of jelly, and I laughed in spite of myself along with them. There was something about witnessing a group of Santas that made it difficult for anyone to resist joining in the fun. Even Kertas gave a short laugh beside me.

Nora Claus had suggested we wait just outside the ring of Santas seated on logs around a roaring fire, the heat melting the snow at their feet. All of them were clad from head to foot, their furs making it clear why they'd chosen to hold their meeting outside in the bracingly cold air. I, too, preferred the star-spangled skies that folks down south would have only associated with nighttime, and I was glad there was an entire ring of people between me and the fire.

Ded Moroz stood above the others, his beard graying but not as white as the snow, hanging from his chin to his waist. His Russian heritage was evident in the firmness of his brow and the paleness of his skin, his mouth closed in a smile, rather than openly laughing. His cerulean blue furs draped from his wrists, the sash about his middle keeping the robes wrapped loosely about his tall frame. The cobalt embroidery reflected the meaning of his name as Grandfather Frost, the turquoise so icy cold to look at, it made me feel right at home. In one hand he held a staff topped with a mesmerizing sapphire, while at his feet sat an ornate lamp, the pale light within competing with the fire's glow.

His granddaughter, Snegurka, nearly took my breath away, so regal did she look in her tall half-moon hat adorning her head, luminescent with enough sparkling aquamarine gems to make Miss Sugar Plum jealous, with two long blonde braids stretching to her knees. As she moved, her shimmering azure and white fur-lined gown seemed to wax and wane like the moon—sometimes as mysterious as midnight, then as incandescent as a peacock's feathers.

She had crossed the circle and was now attempting to shake awake the one her grandfather had called "Noel."

"Papai Noel!" she repeated, her voice tinkling like icicles in the wind.

"Huh? What?" the Brazilian Santa said slowly.

He stretched, and I could see now that someone had thrown a white fur over him, for all he wore was a red t-shirt and shorts, with a Santa cap upon his head. He pulled the fur down to the tips of his white whiskers, his nutmeg face smiling so his eyes crinkled. He reached forward and picked up a pair of sunglasses that had fallen in the snow, replacing them on his face before pulling the furs close once more.

"I'm sorry, dear. I must've dozed off. It's these furs...and the fire...and the glare of the moon off the new-fallen snow. Give me sandy beaches any day of the week."

"It's all right. It's just that Nick wants us to come to a decision so we can call it a day."

"Ah, of course," said Papai Noel, stifling a yawn. "Then we must come to a decision... What decision was that again?"

"Do we need to banish socks and stockings and revert to only shoes being left out," summed up Nick, swilling a mug in his right hand. It was most likely full of warm milk, considering he held a gingerbread biscotti in the other hand. "I think it's time we put it to a vote."

Four hands went up for yay.

Four hands went up for nay.

Four hands went up for undecided.

"You voted twice," Sheng Dan Lao Ren said around a mouthful of apple, pointing at Papai Noel.

"In parts of my country, my children don't wear shoes," Papai Noel complained. "And in other parts of my country, my children don't wear socks *or* shoes. Who am I to vote one way or the other?" He turned to Nick. "Must we really place a moratorium over such a small thing? Does it really matter what the children put out for us to fill?"

"I hear tell you sometimes simply remove the sock, exchanging it for a present, rather than filling it," Father Christmas said in a high British accent, adjusting his pince-nez.

"Have you seen the size of children's socks? How on earth am I supposed to fit anything in six inches square?"

"That's why shoes make far more sense. More 'footage' for gifts." Sinterklaas smiled at his little pun.

"Precisely my point," said Papai Noel, risking a cold hand to wave toward Sinterklaas in gratitude for his endorsement.

"Perhaps, the children could make a point of leaving the one rogue sock that's always missing its mate," said Babbo Natale with an Italian wave of his hand for emphasis. "Then we'd be doing a doubly good service!"

"So long as the sock or shoe is large enough to fit an apple, my sisters won't mind either way." Sheng Dan Lao Ren took another large bite of his apple after he spoke.

"Well, der Weihnachtsmann?" Nick asked, turning to a dark and brooding figure on the far side of the circle. "You're the one who made the motion. What do you think? Can we just drop the issue and continue to let each Santa do it his own way? I know you like things neat and tidy but...it *is* Christmas."

The smoke of the fire blew directly toward the crimson-hooded figure, impairing my view of the German Santa.

He said nothing, but nodded once slowly down and up, then waved his hand in a manner that said, "Let's move on."

"All right then, all those in favor of not changing a thing, raise your hand."

Almost all the hands went up—except for Papai Noel, whose soft snores could be heard once more from across the fire.

"Then that's a gift wrap, folks. Thank you all for coming. I encourage you to enjoy the rest of your day here at the North Pole." Nick began to turn away but then turned back, shaking his mug. "Steer clear of the reindeer, though, would you? They've been a might tetchy lately and I can't make that sleigh fly without them."

"Pausing on the rooftops again are they, Nick?" asked Sinterklaas. "That's why I prefer my horse. Not a problem in a hundred years."

"So you keep telling me," Nick said before taking a swig of milk.

"If anyone would care to join us, we'll be baking some of our traditional goodies at the hotel," Baba Noël offered as he stood and pressed the wrinkles out of his red coat.

"Like what?" Father Christmas asked, his pale cheeks curved beneath his pince-nez.

"Baba's going to teach me how to make *kahk* for starters," Père Noël said, pulling his hood up over his head.

"Need a glass of water? Sometimes milk gives me a frog in my throat, too," said Father Christmas, giving Père a pat on the back.

The French Santa shook his head, but the Egyptian Santa

answered with a laugh, "No, he correctly pronounced it. *Kahk* is an Egyptian Christmas treat. Come by the hotel and I'll give you a taste."

"Will do."

As the Santas began to disperse, Kertas and I smiled and waved at those who passed us, waiting for Nick Claus to notice us waiting to speak with him.

After shaking everyone's hands and covering Papai Noel with another fur, Nick left the fire ring and made a beeline for Nora's side.

He glanced around once, to be sure no one could hear him, before muttering under his breath, "You call this a happy place? Why did we have to have all these Santas?!"

"Because you couldn't have handled the whole world on your own, dear," said Nora. "Do you need a drink?"

"What do you think?" Nick said with a twinkle in his eye.

9

Nick and Nora Claus

It was time to call on dear old Santa Claus, to see what we could see, so we followed the Clauses toward their home, which was just around the corner. The epic home was known for being one of the more magical places in the North Pole, which was saying something.

To some, the house looked like a magnificent red and green present, complete with sparkling bow.

"I've always been told one should live in the Christmas Present," Nick Claus would joke.

To others, the house was a castle, with turrets and wings that extended to either side for days, every window twinkling with a cheery light at all times.

To me it was something unique: a monumental snow globe, with enough snow to keep me cool and comfortable, even when we went inside.

"What does the house look like to you?" I asked Kertas at my side.

He grumbled something under his breath and declined to speak up. I was willing to bet he saw someplace bearing a resemblance to a giant Advent wreath, all five candles aflame.

I wondered what the Clauses saw—perhaps something akin to a semi-subterranean, rectangular building of sod and whalebone, given Nick's Iñupiat heritage. They gave a different answer every time I asked, as changeable as a child's Christmas list, and about as whimsical.

"A successful meeting?" I asked as we walked, Nick and Nora arm in arm.

"It's like herding arctic snow puppets, I tell you." Nick shook his head. "Did Miss Plum find you?"

"Yes, sir, she did. She was right: Tannenbaum was murdered, and what's more, his father died under similar circumstances two years ago."

"Interesting...," Nick murmured, stroking his long beard as white as the snow.

"No, Nicky," Nora said under her breath. "This is not the time to take on a murder investigation. We're only four days out from Christmas, three days from Christmas Eve!"

"I know, I know," he said, pulling open the door to their home.

A swirl of snow greeted me as we entered, and I took a deep breath of fresh, cold air, turning my face upward to catch the cool flakes as they fell.

Ah, this was living.

I could feel all my worries dissipating like stars as the sun rises—or so I've heard, since I've never been alive to see the sun. I wondered what it was like. Was it as large as the moon? As bright? Brighter? The point was it was a new dawn. I felt reenergized, like I had this morning, before Miss Plum showed up and dropped this pinecone of a problem into my lap.

"He can't help now," Nora said, pulling off her scarf and hat and shaking her gray curls. To her, it must not have been snowing inside. "There's a lost reindeer."

"There is?" I asked in surprise. Two cases in one day? Three if you counted the cold case of Ernst Tannenbaum's murder.

"Yes. No one *nose* where Rudolph is!" She laughed at her little pun as she removed her red fur-lined cloak.

"You *sleigh* me, darling," Nick returned, also removing his red and white coat, revealing red and green suspenders pulled tight over a little, round belly. "It's always a Christmas party when you're around."

"Party? I'm a riot!"

Nora made a face at Nick and Nick made one back, then they laughed, kissed, and we finally moved out of the entryway. Kertas grumbled and rolled his eyes at their display of affection. I found it sweet. It was good to know at least one couple in the world was getting along these days.

These days. How could I have thoughts like that when I supposedly didn't remember specifics from my past lives? Once again I wondered if what I'd woken up thinking to be true had been a lie. Perhaps if I tried really hard, I could remember details from last year after all.

I closed my eyes and tried to recall last Christmas. I pictured

Kertas standing with me, a mug of hot cider in his hand, the steam curling off the top, the smell of apples, cinnamon, and nutmeg filling the air. I tried to imagine us competing with Christmas carols. Perhaps it had started with him making that reindeer reference: "If the nose blinks it's probably Rudolph."

And then maybe I'd said, "'With your nose so bright...'"

And then he'd said, "'Westward leading, still proceeding, guide us to thy perfect light...'"

And then I'd said, "'And so it continued both day and night...'"

And then he'd said—

"Hey, Shovel, you all right?" the gnome's growl interrupted my thoughts.

My eyes flew open. "Yeah, yeah, I was just trying to remember."

"Remember what? The first Christmas? You looked like you were trying to stuff an entire Christmas tree up a chimney. You're not the Grinch, you know."

I smiled at the image. How was it I could recall lines to Christmas carols and Christmas movies and yet not be able to actually remember meeting Kertas last year?

I wasn't certain if what I'd just pictured was a memory or me forcing a memory. How did one know the difference?

A question for another time. We had bigger problems at the moment.

As Nora disappeared around the corner, I took the opportunity to nab Nick by the elbow.

"We need your help, Mr. Claus," I said. "If you could shed some light on Ernst Tannenbaum's death, we might be able to also solve the murder of Otmar Tannenbaum."

"You're sure the two are connected?" Nick asked with a frown.

"The coroner found evidence that both of them had been poisoned with mistletoe, and Kertas here was pretty sure Otmar was hot on the heels of his father's murderer."

"I never was able to solve that one...," Nick murmured.

"It seems likely that Otmar was killed because he figured it out, don't you think?" Kertas said softly.

"Please stop trying to distract my Santa," Nora said, suddenly reappearing with a tray of cups and a glass jug. "He's got enough on his mind as it is, what with the big Santa meeting today and the reindeer giving him problems. Besides, he's already on a case."

"He is?" I asked.

"A case of milk." She set down the tray and the white liquid sloshed inside the jug.

"And cookies!" Nick added, heading around the same corner toward what I assumed must be the kitchen.

When he returned, he held out a platter to Kertas, who politely took a tree-shaped cookie, which I thought was a little too on the nose. Nick watched him, obviously waiting for him to take a bite.

Kertas glanced at Nora, but she was busy pouring glasses of milk for the three of them.

The gnome lifted the cookie and took a bite, obviously anticipating a trick of some sort, since Nick was watching him like he expected him to spit it out and shout, "It's full of pepper!"

But Kertas didn't do that. Instead, his face lit up with a glow to rival Christmas tree lights.

"It tastes like homemade skyr!" He took another, much larger bite. "Almost as good as Mother's—though don't tell her I said that." He finished the cookie. "Or worse, don't tell Skyrgamur or you'll never taste another cookie." He reached forward to take another one.

Nick laughed. "Your big brother is welcome to all the cookies he wants. It's Nora's newest secret recipe." He set down the platter, grabbing a reindeer-shaped cookie for himself. "The cookies taste like your favorite thing to eat!"

He handed a snowman-shaped cookie to me. "Here, have a bite."

I took the cookie in surprise. I'd never eaten one before—never eaten anything for that matter. But Nick and Nora were both smiling at me in a way that made me figure I might as well try.

I removed my corncob pipe and stuck the cookie in its place. A sensation occurred not unlike when I "smelled" things. My head was suddenly full of what I supposed to be "taste"—the taste of something I'd always wanted to try based on the smell, but never been able to before.

"Hot cocoa! With marshmallows!" I cried, shoving the cookie farther into my mouth.

"Careful: they go right through you," Nora said with a wink, as the cookie passed through my head and out the back.

Kertas caught it and handed it back to me.

"I always wondered what would happen if a snowman ate one of my cookies," she said with a grin.

"What an amazing invention!" I held the cookie before my eye and turned it this way and that. It looked just like the other cookies on the platter, complete with practically perfect icing decoration, and when I broke it in half, it crumbled like normal.

"I realized not everyone likes sugar cookies." Nora handed a glass of milk to Kertas and then to Nick. "And Nicky was actually getting sick of the flavor—if you can believe it!"

Nick gave Nora a squeeze. "She's the best thing since mistletoe, isn't she?" He stole another kiss. "Which brings us to your little matter. I don't think it would hurt to answer a few questions, my dear. I have a feeling I'll be in for *less* work if I pass on what I know to these fine fellows."

Nora waved the star-shaped cookie in her hand in acceptance before taking a bite.

He turned to me. "As a snowman, I'm sure the winter's rage freezes your blood less coldly, and therefore you'd love a chance at a cold case, but I warn you: this one's so cold it's frozen solid."

10

'Twas Five Nights Before Christmas

"We'd just come back from our annual trip." Nick rested his hands across his belly under his thick white beard. "December 20th—cutting it a little closer than I would have liked, since the next day was the big Santa Meeting. This time of year, I'm a busy man, haven't got time to play, but thanks to the S-ANTA, I haven't felt the usual rush leading up to the denouement, as it were. There was a full moon that year, which I suppose means I should have expected something...unusual."

"Do odd things tend to happen on nights with a full moon?" I asked, glancing at Kertas.

"More like on nights there's no moon," Kertas said. "Like the first year we used Rudolph."

Nora nodded. "Or the time Jack Frost had amnesia and forgot to make it wintertime."

"Or the year the North Pole Express broke down and the visiting children were stranded here for twelve days."

I smiled. "I bet they didn't mind that."

Kertas shook his head. "You'd think, growing up with twelve older brothers, I would have been better prepared for the chaos." He took a fierce bite out of his skyr-flavored sugar cookie. "That song about the twelve days of Christmas? Comes from that year. Let me tell you, when you get all the drummers, pipers, lords, ladies, and every kind of bird together..." He shivered. "I don't know what those Santas were thinking..."

I could only imagine.

"But this time it was a full moon," I said.

"And murder." Nick nodded. "Christmas is supposed to be a time of curling up all comfy and cozy by the fire. Instead, we arrived back late on the twentieth and I was eager to get home to the missus. I just felt in my gut that something must have gone wrong while we were away."

"Franklin, Mr. Tannenbaum's secretary, mentioned you were all out of sorts upon your return. He implied that it might have been the same thing that was the reason behind Mr. Tannenbaum's murder."

Nick stroked his beard. "I doubt that. I was mostly upset because we'd returned home later than I'd expected, and I was missing my wife. Two weeks on the road with no one but Tannenbaum and a bunch of Santas—each convinced their way of doing things is the only way—can make a person feel as tired and old as your grandmother's traditional Christmas tree skirt."

"If you met with all the Santas on the trip, then why have the meeting at the North Pole also?"

"The trip is to check on the S-ANTA, which means we were only visiting those countries that use trees. Not everyone has them yet, and frankly some of the Santas would prefer to keep it that way."

"Was there a particular Santa that seemed more angry than the others?"

Nick frowned. "If you're suggesting that one of our Santas might have gone astray and killed Tannenbaum, I'm going to stop you right there."

I adjusted my pipe in my mouth. That was exactly what I was suggesting, but I didn't want to make Nick holler, "Stop," so I didn't say anything in response.

"Each of those men believe whole-heartedly that they are the myth, the man, the legend. None of them could have, or would have, harmed Tannenbaum. Why would they? He'd helped all of us by inventing the S-ANTA." Nick shook his head. "No, we went over it all back then. There was nothing special about the trip. It must have been something here that was the cause of his death. All I know is, we returned, and he was found dead the next morning."

"Well you're no help at all," Kertas said grumpily, though I was pretty sure he was being sarcastic.

"Nothing special happened on your trip?" I asked. "No crisis averted? No 'Day You Saved Christmas'?"

Nick nibbled at his cookie and shook his head yet again. "Nothing like that. I don't know why Ernst told his son he'd saved Christmas. It's possible he just meant the S-ANTA was working properly. Otmar asked me the same question and I'll give you the same answer: as far as I was concerned, it was just another trip."

"But not just another Christmas," Kertas murmured. "The next morning, his father was dead, and Mr. T was never the same after that."

I rubbed at the spot where the brick had flown through me earlier. I was thankful it hadn't done worse to me than knock me over. From what I'd heard, dying when you weren't a snowman was much worse than what I went through every year, which was more like a fading out, like marshmallows in hot cocoa. I was eternally grateful I didn't have to die every Christmas Day. Instead, I got to enjoy life for twelve days, with Christmas usually featuring as the high point.

"So there's nothing more to it?"

Nick shrugged. "The S-ANTA seemed to be working perfectly and everyone was pleased with the results. I still have to pull on the old boots, red cap, and coat, mind you, but it was getting to the point where I was extending the hours of the night by almost a month in order to get to every child by morning. They say time is relative, and this is especially true for Santa Claus. With the S-ANTA, it feels like things are back to being almost as easy as I imagine it was for Nora's great-great-grandfather when he first started, before more of the world took on the notion of Santa Claus."

"Only two greats?" I asked, turning to Nora. "Didn't St. Nicholas live in the two hundreds?"

"Yes, but how do you remember that?" Nora raised a quizzical eyebrow.

"He's been remembering more details this time around," Kertas put in. "Perhaps one year he'll get to the point where he remembers everything."

I hadn't thought of that. "But you think there might have been someone here, at the North Pole, who could have been behind it?"

"Well..." Nick glanced at Nora before leaning in close to me and Kertas. "Now, don't tell a single soul what I'm going to say."

Kertas and I exchanged glances, then nodded.

"Before we went our separate ways that night, the night before he died, Ernst tried to tell me something. He kept starting and stopping, like he wasn't sure how to say it."

"What *did* he get out?" I asked.

"'Be sure to...'"

"'Be sure to' what?"

"I don't know. That's exactly the problem. We were interrupted by Nora showing up to give me a kiss hello." He wrapped his arm around his wife. "Not that I had any issue with that, of course. But it meant Ernst never got to finish his thought. He probably figured he'd just tell me in the morning."

"Only he was dead."

Nick nodded and ran a hand through his beard. "I've often wondered if whatever he was about to tell me might have saved his life if he had."

"It's not your fault, Nicky," Nora said softly, taking his hand.

"I know, I know. It's just...difficult. The way I see it, I may be the Spirit of Christmas Present, but it's still my job to keep the Christmas spirit in the past, present, *and* future."

"You're not responsible for someone's death."

"I just wish he'd told me. What if all this might have been prevented by the actions of one man?"

"If you insist on looking at it that way, then it's Ernst Tannenbaum's fault for his own death and his son's," said Kertas. "He's the one who didn't tell you what he knew. If he'd let just one other person in on what had happened on that trip, neither of them might have been murdered."

"You're right, you're right. I know you're right." Nick sighed. "I've gone through phases. Not gonna lie. Sometimes I doubt I can go on. But as it so happens, it usually works out that when I'm down, Nora is up, and when Nora is down, I'm feeling up. That's marriage for you. Being there for the other person when they're down." He gave his wife's hand a squeeze and she did the same in return.

"What about when you're both down?"

"Then at least we're down together," said Nora, giving Nick a peck on the cheek for good measure.

"The North Pole is full of magic and wonder. I hate to see that overshadowed by murder," I said sadly.

The other three nodded in agreement as we sat quietly, as though offering up a moment of silence for the loss of what we'd thought was true of where we lived: that it was someplace outside the realism of the rest of the world. But it seemed even the North Pole wasn't safe.

"I can't let it get me down," Nick finally said. "Like they said in *Miracle on 34th Street*, 'Someday you're going to find that your way of facing this realistic world just doesn't work. And when you do, don't overlook those lovely intangibles. You'll discover those are the only things that are worthwhile.'"

"Precisely," agreed Nora, giving Nick's hand another squeeze. "There's always been a magic to gift-giving. From the Biblical gift of God's Son to good old Saint Nick. The first St. Nicholas believed that so wholly, he walked away from his life as a bishop so he could stop arguing church politics and keep doing what God had called him to do: help the needy."

"And he walked all the way to the North Pole?" I asked.

"So Nora's family tells it," said Nick. "He traveled around the world with his family first for a few centuries, then ended up here. Her grandfather was the one who decided it was getting to be too much for him after a couple centuries, so he set up the franchise model. Instead of being 'Santa Claus' for everyone, he picked a new man for each country. Makes things a lot simpler don't you think?"

He swirled his glass of milk. "At least, that was the idea. And for the most part it does work. It's just that, like anything where people are involved, not everyone always agrees."

"What if they spoke with the other Santas?" suggested Nora. "You saw each of them on your trip, didn't you? Maybe one of them knows what Ernst was talking about."

"You're welcome to it." Nick said with a wave of his hand. "Most of them are here, so you might as well. You'll find most of them staying at The Nutcracker Suites downtown."

11

Noël, Noël

"Now mix that all together until it forms a nice dough, and 'voila' as you say. While that sits for an hour, we can work on making the agameya."

Kertas and I followed the sweet smell of honey and cinnamon to the happily lit outdoor kitchen of the local hotel.

Huddled around the kitchen stove were two small, round individuals that could only be a couple of Santas. Their cheeks were nice and rosy from the mix of cold air and heat coming from the oven. One of them was Père Noël and the other was Baba Noël, who was clearly in the process of teaching an Egyptian recipe to the French Santa.

"Making spirits bright with a little baking?" Kertas asked as we approached.

Both Noëls looked up with a smile as we neared.

"Ah, the snowman!" Baba Noël proclaimed. "I was hoping I would have a chance to speak with you again."

He came around the table on which was collected the standard baking ingredients: flour, milk, sugar, as well as honey, pistachios, and cinnamon the color of Baba's skin.

"Again?" I raised an eyebrow.

Baba nodded excitedly. "A few years ago you hit on a Yuletide treasure by recommending I switch out my walnuts for pistachios and I have been making my *kahk* that way ever since." He smiled and shook my twig hand.

I glanced at Kertas. "How would I know what tasted good?"

"I told you the traditional recipe called for walnuts, but I was having a difficult time finding them, so you suggested pistachios—and the rest, as they say, is history!"

Baba's enthusiasm was encouraging, even if I had no recollection of what he was talking about.

"I suppose it's a good thing you're baking outside, then," I said, glancing about at the strings of lights blinking a bright red and green. "So that I could share my brilliance."

The breath of the Santas and Kertas crystalized in the air against the night sky as they laughed.

"I do have to ask, though. What is *kahk*? I'm guessing it's some sort of cookie."

"Why don't you tell him, Père. I seem to have misplaced the wooden press mold... I'll be back in a moment," Baba said, giving Père a pat on the back before whisking away toward his hotel room.

The French Santa nodded and turned to me, grooming his long white whiskers as he did so. His beard was shorter than Nick's, but his mustache was longer, bending in a W-shape across his upper lip and curving under his pale cheeks. I saw he kept his white hair shorter atop his head when he pulled back the hood of his red cloak trimmed in white fur.

"It is getting warm out here with that oven. Will you be all right?" he asked kindly.

"I'll be fine so long as I keep to this side, I think," I said, waving to the table between us.

"*Bon.*" Père picked up a glass of wine and swirled it gently before taking a sip.

"No milk to go with your cookies?"

"*Quelle horreur!* A grown man does not drink milk. I prefer a glass of red with my treats, thank you." He saluted me with his glass before taking another, longer drink. "*Bon,* we are currently making *kahk*, which Baba tells me is a traditional Egyptian cookie he cannot eat until after January 6th, though he has kindly offered to show me how to make them today since we are together and he is in no rush to return home."

"Will you be heading home soon?"

"I head out tomorrow. Half of my country has already been visited, though I am known as Saint Nicholas to them."

"'Jolly Old Saint Nicholas, lean your ear this way,'" I quoted.

"Precisely."

"How's that donkey of yours?" Kertas asked, pouring himself a glass of wine to join Père.

"Gui is well, though he has had to cut back on the apples this year, much to his dismay, reduced to eating hay out of a lowly manger. The S-ANTA has been beneficial in more ways than one for us, as less travel has meant he is less likely to come across a tree decorated with the fruit."

"Apples rather than candy canes?" I asked.

"Apples were decorating trees long before those sugary things," Père said with a wave of his hand. "It is a great reminder of the Garden of Eden."

"I don't think that particular fruit was an apple," Kertas said.

Père shrugged. "It is tradition."

I wondered what Mrs. Cane would say to that.

"It has always been beneficial to divide my duties between two dates twenty days apart," Père continued. "The S-ANTA has made it so my deliveries on Christmas Eve are quite negligible. Even with the increase in gifts each year, I simply flick the switch to have the presents appear beneath the tree. The smaller gifts can still fit in the shoes, so long as they are nearby."

"What did you think about der Weihnachtsmann's idea of enforcing the use of shoes vs. socks this year?"

"My children have always set out shoes, so it would make no difference to us," said the French Santa. "I find shoes to be generally the perfect size for fitting a small chocolate or toy within. I do not see the draw toward socks, myself."

"How's that old Le Père Fouettard?" Kertas asked. "Still up to his usual tricks?"

Père focused on his drink, then muttered, "I think I will go see if I can help Baba find that mold."

He disappeared before I could question his avoidance of Kertas's question, so I turned to the gnome instead.

"Who is Le Père Fouettard?"

"So you noticed his lack of interest in discussing the black-hearted scoundrel, as well?" Kertas frowned. "Fouettard has been a counterpart of Père's going back centuries. He's usually to be seen, if he's seen at all, dressed in black with a whip in his hand for punishing misbehaving children."

I raised my brows in surprise.

"Oh, don't worry, he's been retired for decades. Parents aren't interested in beating the bad out of their children these days."

Thankfully, I thought. "What about coal?"

Kertas shook his head. "Even that's gone by the wayside. The only time I've seen coal in kids' stockings is as a joke, or when the gift is a bag of charcoal to help naturally air out a bedroom or closet, or to be used on a grill."

"Or to build a snowman," I said with a wink. "This Fouettard fellow sounds like the type who might be behind a murder."

Kertas nodded. "That's what I was thinking, too, which is why I asked. But Père seemed reticent to discuss—"

"Here it is. I knew I'd packed it." Baba said, waving a wooden press as he returned with Père at his side. "Now we can begin making the filling."

He set down the press and clapped his hands together, rubbing them in anticipation. "This is my favorite part. So, first, we need to melt the butter. You do that, Père, and I'll measure the flour. We'll whisk the flour in the pan once the butter is melted. Then we just remove it from the heat to add the honey and pistachios and sesame seeds. Then back onto the heat, stirring until it thickens, then back off the heat to cool until we can form it into small balls. By then the dough should have rested enough and we'll be able to start putting it all together."

Père nodded and turned to the oven.

"So, what brought you two together this fine afternoon?" Baba asked as he measured out the flour and turned to give it to Père.

"We're tracking down the murderer of Mr. Tannenbaum," I said.

A crash came from behind Baba.

"*Je suis désolé*," Père muttered. "I dropped the flour. Would you mind measuring that again for me?"

"Too much wine, my friend?" Baba joked. "Not a problem. Here you go." He chuckled as he measured and handed the flour back to Père. "Not the first time the flour has gone everywhere while making *kahk*!"

"Another good reason to be cooking outside," I said. It was a wonder all kitchens weren't set up this way. The cold air must have felt good compared to the heat of the stovetop, and not just to me. "Père said you're not due back until January."

Baba nodded. "That's right. In Egypt, Christmas Day is January 7th, depending on your religious affiliation, though really we start celebrating and counting down to Christmas on November 25th, which begins the Coptic month of Kiahk."

"Wow. You celebrate Christmas for that long?"

"Forty-three days of Advent. Who doesn't wish Christmas lasted a whole month? Why, in America I hear Christmas is sometimes celebrated starting as far back as before Halloween."

"But don't you have to eat, or not eat, a certain way that whole time?" Père asked, bringing the combined butter and flour to the table so the nuts, seeds, and honey could be added.

"We call it the Holy Nativity Fast, and yes, we eat a vegan diet for that month, fasting away as the old year passes, in recognition and remembrance of the night of our dear Savior's birth, when the Lord came to this earth to die for us. It is the least we can do."

"I don't think I could go that long without *magret de canard, coq au vin,* or *Châteaubriand.*" Père shook his head, then returned the mixture to the stovetop.

"Ah, but then we celebrate after service on Christmas Eve with a big meal! Food tastes so much better when it has been denied a long while. My favorite is the *fata*—a lamb soup with rice and garlic. And, of course, the *kahk*."

"So you deliver your presents on January 6th?"

"Yes, and it is only in recent years that my people have begun to use Christmas trees as part of the celebration, so I am still usually to be found climbing in through windows to leave presents in exchange for *kahk,* rather than relying on the S-ANTA." Baba peeked over Père's shoulder. "That looks about right. It's time to roll up our sleeves and then roll up some balls."

"Have you spoken to Sinterklaas? He's done with his deliveries, too," Père said. "I just saw him heading toward the stables."

I wondered why Père seemed eager to get rid of us. Perhaps he worried we weren't done asking him about his friend in black.

"I'll be teaching Baba how to make *pain d'épice* next. It's my personal recipe. By the time you're done talking with Sinterklaas, I bet we'll have a couple different treats for you to try."

12

Sinterklaas Kapoentje

"*Een goed paard... Een goed paard...*"

"What's he saying?" I asked as we approached the stable and found Sinterklaas brushing down a large, powerfully built white horse.

"'Good horse,' I think," said Kertas quietly.

"It's certainly a beautiful one."

The horse was as white as a lily flower, lean and lank, with a soft coat clearly well-loved and well-fed. As we neared, his gray muzzle lifted and he looked straight at us.

"Hello!" I called.

Sinterklaas turned from where he stood, one hand on the horse's halter, the other holding a brush aloft, his stately red robes dusting the straw-covered ground. He'd tied up his long, thin white beard, most likely so that it wouldn't get in the way. His ceremonial shepherd's staff, which he'd had when we'd last seen him around the fire, was leaning against the wall of one of the box stalls on the right.

"Hallo!" the Dutch Santa responded.

"Your horse is beautiful," I said, respectfully maintaining my distance as Sinterklaas gave the horse a pat.

"He's the only pure white Dutch Warmblood in the entire world. I'm lucky to have him as my companion."

"Hello, Amerigo," Kertas said, and it took me a minute to realize he was talking to the horse.

"Heeeey there, Kertas," the horse whinnied with a shake of his mane.

Kertas walked up to him and gave him a good head-butt, like they were goats or dwarves.

"How've you been? Good year down there?"

The horse pawed the ground. "Good enough. Not enough carrots."

"Now, now, Amerigo," said Sinterklaas. "I know for a fact you received more carrots this year than last year. It's a carrot-strophe."

Ignoring what was no doubt his tenth pun of the day, I turned from Sinterklaas to his horse and said, "I'm sure you're making fewer in-person deliveries than normal, thanks to the S-ANTA, so that might account for the feeling that there were fewer carrots left out for you overall."

"The S-ANTA?" Amerigo frowned.

"We don't use the S-ANTA," Sinterklaas said, explaining

his horse's confusion. "My helpers are unionized, so there's no replacing them now."

I nodded. "The elves are unionized around here, too."

"My helpers aren't elves, they're Piets. Folks sometimes call them 'Sooty Piets' because they're small enough to fit down chimneys, so I don't have to. Amerigo and I simply clip-clop over the rooftops, waving to all the good little girls and boys. The Piets are also the ones keeping track of the naughty and nice in the Big Book, determining whether the children get presents or get stuffed in a sack and taken to Spain for a year to teach them a lesson." Sinterklaas laughed to himself at this. "Of course, the Piets would never actually do that. I don't condone kidnapping. Just a little rumor we put about to encourage better behavior from the kids."

"I don't blame the Piets for joining the union," interrupted Amerigo. "They're the ones who do all the work. And they haven't always been the best...represented."

"I agree," said Sinterklaas, going back to brushing. "It's a good thing you caught me. My boat leaves tomorrow. It's back to Spain for me and Amerigo."

"Spain? I thought you were from the Netherlands."

Sinterklaas shook his head. "I visit the Netherlands from the second Saturday of November until *Sinterklaasavond* on December 5th, traveling from town to town making my deliveries, but I live the rest of the year in Madrid, Spain."

"Why Spain?"

"Why the North Pole?" he returned with a shrug. "It's where I'm based."

A loud snuffling sound made me turn to find Amerigo

sniffing at Kertas. "You smell like cinnamon," he said appreciatively.

"We just came from Père Noël and Baba Noël baking cookies," Kertas explained.

"Oooo, are they making *pepernoten*?" Sinterklaas asked.

"Or *kruidnoten*?" Amerigo asked.

"Or *speculaas*?"

"Or *banketletter*?"

"None of those," said Kertas. "They're making *kahk.*"

"Ah, is it made with flour, butter, sugar..." The horse gave Kertas's hat another good snuff until Kertas batted him away. "...and cinnamon?"

Kertas and I exchanged a look.

"Yes," the gnome said slowly. "And honey."

Amerigo nodded. "Not unlike our *pepernoten*, then. Just switch out the honey for aniseed."

"And add some cloves," said Sinterklaas. "Like all good spiced cookies at this time of year."

I had to agree. There was something about the smell of gingerbread spices—that lovely mix of nutmeg, cloves, cinnamon, ginger, cardamom, and more—that just smelled like Christmas.

"I'm partial to mince pies myself," said a new voice.

I thought perhaps another horse in the stables had joined the conversation, but then turned to find it was none other than Father Christmas himself.

"Might sound unappetizing to your stomachs, but in Denmark, Danish children leave out rice pudding, so at least I get something better than that." Adjusting his pince-nez, the

British Santa approached, a sack over his back that I assumed was full of presents.

"Don't forget the glass of sherry," Kertas said with a wink, offering his hand in greeting.

"I'd prefer a Guinness, honestly," said Father Christmas. "Ireland's usually ready with a glass to hand, and Australia always goes for beer over milk, given the time of year for them."

"What about New Zealand?" I asked.

"I don't visit New Zealand, I'm afraid. That's Hana Kōkō's territory. Sometimes we get together to share a bit of pavlova, though. I hear he gets beer and pineapple from his children."

"Did Mr. O. Tannenbaum ever speak with you about it? Specifically about the pōhutukawa tree? Kertas mentioned Otmar had been considering trading in a winter Christmas for a summer one."

Father Christmas nodded. "Indeed, we did discuss New Zealand and Australia a few times. Nick told me you're working to solve his murder." He shook his head. "I was sorry to hear he'd passed. He will be missed." He turned to Kertas. "Do you know who'll be taking over the tree business?"

"Not yet."

"I wouldn't be surprised if it ended up being you. After all, you've been at his elbow for a long time now."

"You bet your boots," said the gnome. "Nearly one hundred years and not a bonus in sight. But I donno." He removed his hat and rubbed his head. "I don't think I'm cut out for running a business. Don't mind assisting, but running's a whole 'nother matter."

Amerigo nodded his head. "I hear you, buddy, I hear you."

"Do you even know how to run the S-ANTA?" I asked, realizing I hadn't done so yet.

Kertas put his hat back over his ears and nodded. "For the most part. It's the business side of things I don't care for. Maybe I could just hire a secretary to do that part for me."

"Like Franklin?" I joked.

Kertas didn't even deign to reply. I knew that turkey was more likely to end up as dinner quicker than a pig walking in on Easter Day.

"Headed back?" Sinterklaas asked, coming around Amerigo to shake hands with his counterpart.

Father Christmas nodded. "It is time. Don't tell them yet, but I've got a satchel full of carrots for the reindeer if they can get me home in less than an hour." He shook the bag over his shoulder.

Amerigo perked up. "Carrots, you say?" he whinnied.

"If Sinterklaas says it's all right..."

The Dutch Santa waved his hand and Father Christmas pulled out a large carrot for the horse.

"Here you go, Amerigo. Happy Christmas!"

"*Vrolijk Kerstfeest*!" Amerigo called out between carrot crunches.

"*Prettige Kerst*!" Sinterklaas echoed.

Father Christmas disappeared farther into the stables, headed toward the stalls that housed his reindeer, who were no doubt hanging with Nick Claus's bunch.

"Hope his reindeer haven't been picking up any bad habits," Kertas muttered, watching the British Santa as I had done.

"Why would they?" I asked.

"From what I hear, Claus's reindeer have a tendency to

get carried away when it comes to the games portion of the evening. Rudolph, especially, has been developing a bit of a gaming habit."

"How'd you hear about that?"

"Mr. T told me."

I raised a brow. "Did he now? And how did *he* come to hear about it?"

"If you're wondering whether he knew because he, too, enjoyed a flutter now and then," Kertas gave me a look, "you'd be spot on. Not only that, but I know he owed those antlered fiends quite a bit."

I moved my pipe from one side of my mouth to the other. "Maybe we've been wrong this whole time." I removed my pipe and tapped it against my hand. "Maybe his death has nothing to do with his father's murder. Maybe it has more to do with a red-nosed reindeer."

13

Reindeer Games

I'd heard none of the other reindeer liked to let Rudolph in on their games, but the way Kertas told it, that was more for Rudolph's benefit than out of any spite the other reindeer held against him. You would have thought the glowing red nose was a tell, but apparently it was the opposite.

"Your Christmas Eve is about to get a bit foggier, so foggy it'll go down in history. Fog as thick as—"

"Peanut butter snaps! You've got to be kidding me!"

Although the stable doors were flung wide open, letting cool air in so I didn't feel overheated, it was quickly apparent the heat was on in the gaming stall.

"I can't help it. The cards were dealt, and I ended up on top."

"Who would've thought you'd go down in history, not for your nose, but for your luck at cards," Kertas said as we came around the corner.

"Kertas!" the reindeer yelled in chorus.

A wild shuffling occurred and suddenly we were surrounded by eight reindeer.

"Hey, buddy, how've you been?"

"Heard about your boss—what a tragedy."

"What happened to Mr. T?"

"He was found dead in the trees, man."

"Brutal."

"So, how're you hanging in there, Kertas?"

The gnome shrugged. "Oh, y'know. I'm hanging 'bout like the annual stocking. This is Shovel. He's helping me solve the mystery of who killed Mr. T."

"Shovel? Like the thing we use to clean the stalls?" the reindeer guffawed, trading knowing looks with the others.

"Grow up, Donder."

"The name's Sam Shovel, like the spade," I said with a tip of my fedora.

"Cool, cool. Nice to meet you. I'm Blitzen." The reindeer offered his hoof. "That's Dasher, Dancer, Prancer, Vixen, Comet, Cupid, Donder, and, of course, you probably have heard of 'the most famous reindeer of all,'" Blitzen said, curving his hooves in quotation marks.

"Cut it out, Blitzen," said Rudolph, rising from the table.

Before his seat I couldn't help but notice there was quite a stack of carrot circles, peppermint rounds, and licorice sticks, no doubt being used as payment for the game.

"Sick of the song already?" Kertas asked.

"Every year people start singing it earlier and earlier. This year I heard it on one radio station in the middle of September! I mean, bouncing bumbles, it wasn't even Halloween yet!"

"Care to join us for a game? We've got room for a couple more players now the Brits left," asked Blitzen, returning to his seat and shuffling the cards on the table.

Don't ask me how a reindeer shuffles cards with hooves. All I know is, the North Pole is a magical place and that's what he was doing.

"What're you playing?" Kertas asked.

"Five card draw," said Donder, coming to stand behind Blitzen. "I'm out. I'd pay to see you beat Rudolph, though, Kertas."

The other reindeer nodded their heads.

"You'll have to remind me how to play, but you can deal me in," I said, sidling up to the table.

Prancer walked me through the basics and Kertas gave me a wink. "It's just for fun," he said reassuringly, though I could tell he was eager to play.

"What're you bringing to the table?" Rudolph asked.

Kertas took a seat. "If I win, I get to ask you a few personal questions."

Rudolph raised an eyebrow. "About what?"

"About Mr. T and his penchant for gambling."

Rudolph smiled and his nose glowed red.

"I'd answer you for free," said Comet.

Rudolph waved a hoof. "Nah, nah, it makes it more fun this way. I'll answer one question from whoever wins."

"Me, too?" Blitzen asked.

"Anyone. Any question. And if I win, I get to ask you a question instead. Deal?"

"Deal," said Kertas, and I nodded in agreement.

Blitzen dealt and I picked up my five cards between my sticks. Two pair of threes and sixes, and a Jack of clubs.

Rudolph took one card, Kertas took two cards, I took one card, and Blitzen took three.

"All right, since we're only betting questions, let's see 'em," said Blitzen.

Rudolph revealed two pairs. "Queens over fours," he said, laying them out.

Kertas was next. "We Three Kings," he said proudly.

I showed my two pairs, then Blitzen flipped his hand to reveal he had squat except a high Ace.

"Not a bad start. All right, ask away," Rudolph said to Kertas.

Kertas looked to me and I nodded reassuringly.

"How much money did Mr. T owe you from his gambling losses?"

Rudolph sat back and flipped a peppermint into his mouth. "Unfortunately, he owed quite a bit, had been stuck in a long losing streak. Now, normally we play for treats." He waved toward the stacks in front of him. "But Mr. T wanted to play for cash. He said he needed spending money that was off the business books."

"For what?"

Rudolph shook his head. "That's another question. Gotta win to ask."

We played another round and Blitzen pulled out ahead with two pairs of sevens over sixes.

"What did Mr. T need the extra cash for?" he asked, giving Kertas a wink as if to say he had our backs.

Rudolph grinned. "For his lady friend, the fairy."

"Miss Sugar Plum?" I asked.

Rudolph nodded, though it had technically been an extra question.

Another round, and this time Rudolph held three Queens. Kertas and I waited to see what he'd ask us.

"How come you've backed out of our games, Kertas? It's been awhile since you've played with us."

"It was getting too hot for me," said the gnome. "I prefer a candle flame to a bonfire. And when I learned the boss was getting in too deep, I knew I'd made the right choice."

It was my turn to deal. I did so, giving myself a hand so lousy I took three cards, and then I hit a bit of luck. Turned out the seven of diamonds I'd kept, along with the four of clubs, went well with my new eight of hearts, six of clubs, and five of diamonds.

"Straight," I called, laying them out quite happily.

"Lords a-leaping, that's a good hand," said Blitzen appreciatively.

"So, Rudolph, tell me, why did you meet with Mr. Tannenbaum last night at the far corner of his Christmas tree farm?"

Kertas looked surprised by my question, but Rudolph didn't.

He nodded, his nose glowing softly. "I know it's against the rules to ask a question, but how did you figure that out?"

"There were hoof prints near the body." I skimmed over the fact that the ones I'd seen might actually have been made by the moose coroner when he'd come to collect the body, rather than a reindeer. I'd figured it was worth a shot in the dark to be direct with the gambler, in the hopes of getting at the truth quicker.

"Could have been put there by anyone," said Rudolph with a shrug. "But since I have nothing to hide, yes. I did meet with Mr. T last night. He wanted to meet with me to find out if I'd be willing to agree to an...alternate source of payment. Rather than cash, he wanted to switch to something else."

The reindeer paused, working on the peppermint in his mouth.

"Enough with the games, Rudolph," said Kertas, standing to his feet, which put him level with the table. "What did he offer you? And more importantly, was it not good enough for you? Did you decide it would be better to take his life in payment?"

"Who do you think I am? Vito Corleone? I'm Santa's lead reindeer. I'm not just a whimsical figure with a glowing nose who affects a jolly demeanor. I'm a symbol. A symbol of Christmas. I don't go around offing people. This is the North Pole, not New York City, for Santa's sake."

"Well then, what did he offer you?"

Rudolph smiled. "He offered me all the carrots I could eat for a full year. Sounded like a good deal to me. We shook on it and I left."

Kertas's eyes narrowed.

"And when I left, he was still alive," added Rudolph, raising his forelegs in defense. "I promise, I didn't kill him. Why would I do that? Now I'm out a year's worth of carrots!"

With all this talk of carrots, I was starting to worry about my nose. Maybe I'd been wrong to walk into this large group of reindeer with my particular choice of nose-wear.

14

Smells Like Christmas

"Did someone say, 'No carrots for Christmas?'"

I turned, expecting this last remark to have been made by one of the reindeer, and was surprised to find we'd been joined by a newcomer with a platter of carrot-shaped cookies that smelled more like ginger than carrots.

"Merry!" the reindeer chorused again, encircling the Gingerbread Man.

"As in 'Merry Christmas'?" I asked.

He gave a licorice-shaped grin. "You got it! I changed my name in the '60s from 'Lebkuchen.' It's difficult to keep a business running when no one can pronounce your name properly."

"Are those delicious-smelling treats for us?" Dancer asked hopefully, his nose almost touching the cookie nearest him.

"They're for my favorite reindeer!" Merry said, then clarified after seeing the disappointed looks on the reindeer around him. "You're *all* my favorites!"

The reindeer seemed pleased by this and helped themselves to a cookie or three.

"'Lebkuchen'—does that mean you're German?" I asked over the sounds of crunching.

Merry shook his head. "Gingerbread has been around for centuries, but legend has it that gingerbread *men* actually began when Queen Elizabeth I asked her cooks to create ginger biscuits in edible likenesses of her favorites at court. So I suppose I'm like most of us: a little bit of this, a little bit of that, both English and German."

"I didn't know you joined the reindeer for their games," Kertas said, waving a carrot-shaped cookie. "Good eats, though."

"Oh, no, I don't have time for games. Especially this time of year! I just popped by with some treats. Testing out a new carrot-gingerbread recipe."

"There's carrot in this?" Kertas asked suspiciously.

"You wouldn't have known it without my saying so, would you?" Merry said with a grin.

"Genius. Perhaps more parents will encourage their kids to eat cookies if they're really sneaking in veggies."

"Precisely my thought," said the Gingerbread Man.

"You must be doing well," I said. "I passed your house earlier today. Looked bigger than last year's."

"Yes, the industry's been booming lately. I recently added an entire addition just for an assembly line for applying gumdrop buttons." He adjusted his own buttons as he said this.

"We just left Père Noël and Baba Noël baking cookies, too."

"Yes, almost every country has a spiced cookie of some sort. Much like Mr. Tannenbaum," he nodded to Kertas, "we've got enough fingers in enough cookie jars to last us a lifetime. No worries of being run out of business here!" Merry waved his empty hand at the now-empty platter.

Merry certainly seemed to live up to his name. He took a moment to make the rounds with the reindeer, asking them what they thought of the cookie and if they had any critiques. His jolliness showed as he patted shoulders and smiled genially.

"He always has a smile on his face," said Kertas, wiping the crumbs from his beard, "even if it's been made of candy ever since that accident with the boiling hot gumdrops."

"Oh?" I asked.

"Merry's not had an easy life, that's for certain. Like the very cookies he's known for, he's been put together piece by piece. He wasn't always the Gingerbread Man. Once upon a time, he was just a man."

"Really?"

Kertas nodded. "It started when his grandmother was run over by a reindeer one Christmas Eve. Frau Perchta wasn't the most well-loved person in the North Pole, but Merry took it hard, as is only natural."

"Why wasn't she liked?"

"She had a tendency to be a bit...finicky when it came to cleanliness. She'd keep a long knife hidden under her ragged skirt, and folks said she'd disembowel you and replace your guts with rocks and straw if your house was a mess."

I adjusted my scarf nervously. "Good grief. She sounds worse than Krampus."

"Funny you should say that. The two of them used to be really close. Anyway, you can imagine it couldn't have been easy for Merry growing up with someone like that, but he loved her all the same. The night of the accident, he couldn't save her. He was hurt himself—lost his leg—but the bakers made him a new one." He waved toward the man now completely made of gingerbread cookie. "He was so grateful to the gingerbread industry for fixing him, that he decided to dedicate his life to it. He's had a couple more accidents along the way, but each time, he's been able to patch it up with gingerbread."

I shook my head in amazement. "I assumed he was just like me—made one Christmas with just enough special magic to come to life." I patted my snowy belly.

Kertas nodded. "Understandable, but in this case, not the same. He's had a rough life, but sometimes that's just the way the cookie crumbles."

I winced at Kertas's pun. He was getting as bad as Nora Claus.

"I'm headed back to the factory," Merry said, coming to shake our hands in farewell. "I'd suggest you stop by sometime to see how it all works, but I don't think you could handle the heat." He smiled at me. "Literally. Those ovens are constantly baking at 350 degrees Fahrenheit or more."

I agreed but thanked him for the offer. "Perhaps I'll peek in a window the next time I pass by. If I don't see you, have a merry Christmas and a happy new year."

"You, too," he said, and left with his platter.

"What a nice guy," said Blitzen, coming up beside me. "So,

are you guys finished with your questions? Can we get back to our real games now? We've only got a few more days till Christmas so this is our last day to relax before the final push."

"Or pull, in our case. Since we pull the sleigh," said Prancer with a wink.

"Yes, yes, you can get back to your game," said Kertas, before turning to me. "I don't think there's much more to learn here, do you? I have a feeling there's no reason why Rudolph might have killed Mr. T."

"Did the older Mr. T ever gamble?" I asked.

Prancer answered for Kertas. "Ernst wouldn't be caught dead at one of our games," he said.

"What about being caught dead *after* one of your games?"

"It was a sad day when he died," Rudolph said, poking his shiny nose into the conversation. "Otmar was never the same after his father passed. Played our games a little less strategically, if you know what I mean. His father's death is the reason why he got up to his neck in IOUs in the first place. He became reckless. Kept betting 'all in' on cards that were clearly not in his favor."

Something occurred to me. "Rudolph, did you reindeer take the Tannenbaums and Nick when they went on their annual S-ANTA check-up trips?"

Rudolph shook his head. "I didn't. That was Vixen and Cupid's job. Nick said he only needed two for the trip since it was just the two of them going, not him and a bag full of gifts that never gets lighter." He turned and beckoned toward two smaller reindeer with short antlers. "Ladies, these gentlemen have a few questions for you."

"Ladies?" I murmured to Kertas. "They have antlers." It

was only then I realized the reindeer I'd been playing cards with had been missing their curved, pointed headwear.

"Males shed their antlers in early December, but females keep theirs year-round," Kertas muttered back. "I think it's something to do with lightening the load before they start making Christmas deliveries."

I'd probably learned this every year, but then, it wasn't really one of those facts worth keeping note of in my notebook.

The two female reindeer joined Kertas and I as the others went back to the table to play another round of poker.

"How can we help you?" Vixen asked, batting her eyelashes at me like she was Clarice from the claymation movie about the red-nosed reindeer.

"Rudolph says you two pulled the sleigh when Nick and the Tannenbaums would travel the Milky Way to check on the S-ANTA."

The reindeer nodded.

"It's been our job since its invention fifty years ago," said Cupid.

I whistled. "I thought reindeer only lived for fifteen years or so."

"If you haven't noticed, time moves a little differently around here," said Vixen with a wink. "We're older than we look."

"You look good for your age," Kertas said appreciatively, and I assumed he was probably just flattering the girls, which seemed to be working, since they giggled and batted their lashes all the more.

"We're interested in hearing about two trips in particular," I said. "The trip before Ernst Tannenbaum's death, and then this one, before the death of Otmar. Was there anything unusual that happened on either trip?"

Vixen and Cupid exchanged glances.

"Not that I can think of," said Vixen.

"Nor I," said Cupid.

A lot of help they were. No one seemed to recall anything unusual ever happening in the North Pole. Perhaps because there was such an inordinate amount of unusual things happening, something usual would be unusual.

"What about usual?" I asked, following the thought. "Can you give us an overview of the trips?"

"I'll tell you what I can," said Cupid. "The trip crossed several countries and continents, and we'd stop along the way to check on the S-ANTA anywhere there were Christmas trees. It didn't matter the type—whether it was palm trees or fir trees, pink trees or aluminum trees."

"We checked on the living and the dead, so to speak." Vixen nodded.

"Do you remember which Santas were visited, and this time I mean the men, not the trees?"

"Too many to name." Cupid's ears twitched. "I'm sure Nick has a list. He always went with whichever Mr. Tannenbaum was going that year."

"Did they alternate?" I looked to Kertas, assuming he knew the answer to this question just as well.

"Yeah, but not according to any pattern or anything," said Kertas. "It was completely random. So if you're thinking someone planned something based on which Tannenbaum was coming through, there'd be no way for them to do so too far out. They'd only find out which one was coming once the sleigh left the North Pole."

"If it was a Santa toward the end of the trip, they'd have more time to prepare," I pointed out. "Was there a general direction of travel?"

"North to south, west to east, and back again." Vixen shrugged.

"Who was the last Santa to be visited this year?"

"Actually, the same as was visited two years prior with Mr. Ernst Tannenbaum," said Vixen, looking to Cupid, who nodded. "Babbo Natale, the Italian Santa."

15

The Luster of Midday

Babbo Natale and Papai Noel were "sunning" themselves in an area where the snow lay round about deep and crisp and even. So brightly shone the moon tonight, that the reflected moonlight bounced more gloriously than ever off the snow, dispelling the shadows of the night.

This time, Papai Noel wasn't hiding under a thick fur, but was instead displaying his red t-shirt and shorts for all to see, a reflector held under his nutmeg face so that the moonbeams hit him with more brilliance where he lay upon a cot. Babbo's pale face beside him was already redder than it had been around the fire, the reflective heat starting to burn his cheeks and tip of his nose. Who knew you could get moon-burn?

Papai lifted his sunglasses as we approached, the crunch of our steps in the snow giving us away.

"Hello, there!" I called out warmly.

"*Ciao*!" called Babbo Natale.

I looked at Kertas, confused. "Does he want us to leave already? I thought '*ciao*' meant 'goodbye'?"

Babbo must have overheard me because he sat up as we neared. "No, no, my friend. '*Ciao*' also means hello. '*Arrivederci*' means farewell, though sometimes we also say '*ciao.*' It is a common expression among friends, as if to say, 'We will see each other once again very soon.' Yes?" His hands waved in the air as he spoke, adding emphasis to his words.

"Let us skip the hellos and goodbyes and instead say, '*Feliz Natal*'!" Papai said.

"Or '*Buon Natale*,' as the case may be." Babbo said with a further wave of his hand.

Rather than argue the point, I commented, "A fine night for moon-bathing!"

"Indeed it is," said Babbo, though he politely set his reflector down beside his cot so as to converse with us further.

"Are Italy and Brazil warmer this time of year?"

"Depends on the part of the country," said Babbo Natale. "The northern parts of Italy can be rather bleak in midwinter, with either frosty wind or days in the single digits—Celsius, of course—while the southern tip near Sicily may be as warm as in the teens or twenties."

"It is the same in Portugal," said Papai Noel. "Which is why I split my time between there and Brazil, where December is the beginning of the hot season, with heavy rain and humidity giving us beautiful days in the upper twenties and thirties." He sighed happily. "I am pleased to have been placed where it is warmer. I do not think I would have thrived so in the North Pole." He shivered at the thought.

"So I take it you don't have any living snowmen where you are from, either of you?" I asked.

They both shook their heads.

"I don't believe there are any living snowmen anywhere in the world except for up here," said Kertas.

I nodded sadly. And with only one of us coming to life at a time, it could be a remarkably lonely existence. I was pleased to have met up with Kertas this time around. It was a nice feeling knowing he was always beside me. I was glad we'd crossed paths again, even if under terrible circumstances.

"We just heard about Mr. Tannenbaum's death," said Babbo. "I was sorry to hear it, and so soon after the death of his father. I take it you are on the case?"

"Have I solved a mystery for you before? Sometimes my memory's a little sloshy between years," I said apologetically, touching my fedora.

Babbo shook his head. "I just remember you asking around last year when Nora Claus's candlesticks went missing." He eyed Kertas. "I take it you found the culprit."

"Yes, he gave me a good talking to and I returned them, if that's what you're wondering." Kertas gave a sheepish smile and shrugged. "What can I say? It's difficult to break a century-long habit."

"Ah, I understand," said Babbo empathetically. "Traditions are traditions for a reason. It is tradition for my counterpart, La Befana, to make the deliveries of the presents on the 5th of January, leaving dried fruit and candy in the children's socks, but since the Christmas trees are set up from December to January, I believe even she will eventually cave to the necessity and expedience of using the S-ANTA to assist in deliveries. Though I don't believe either of us will ever completely hand over our work to a machine."

Kertas nodded. "I don't think that was ever Mr. T's intention. He didn't want to replace Santa, he only wanted to help you, since the exponential increase in the number of children and, thereby, deliveries, will only become greater over time."

"My countries still do not fully embrace the tree," said Papai, adjusting his sunglasses. "They are more likely to set up a nativity scene than a tree, though the trees are becoming more popular as additions to the scene."

"The people of my country do the same," said Babbo. "I pray the nativity will always be a part of the Christmas celebration. Do your families wait to add the baby Jesus to the scene until Christmas Eve?"

Papai nodded. "Of course! The nativity is set up on December 8th with Mary and Joseph, angels, shepherds, sheep, and other animals in the stable, but Jesus cannot be laid in his manger until December 24th—usually without the little ones knowing, so that it is as much a surprise for them as the presents that seem to appear when they return from Midnight Mass."

Birds of a feather, these two, I thought.

"And later, on the night of Epiphany, we add the three kings bearing gifts after traversing afar. To us, Christmas is a celebration of our faith, more than a celebration of Santa Claus."

I nodded. "You said you have someone who helps you, Babbo—La Befana? Is she here with you?"

Babbo shook his head. "She does not usually join me on my

trips north. Although she is sometimes painted as a witch of sorts, she is more like my great-aunt. The two of us have been sharing the load of deliveries for centuries now. It is she who delivers gifts on the night of Epiphany, whilst I deliver them on Christmas Eve."

"So the children of Italy have multiple times when they open gifts?"

"Yes. It spreads the joy of Christmas out across the weeks. And makes it easier for La Befana and I to share the load, without the S-ANTA's help."

It was clear Babbo was quite defensive when it came to the S-ANTA's involvement. I wondered if he were pushed...

I snapped my branchy fingers. "I knew I'd heard the word 'nativity' somewhere before. It was in relation to Mr. Tannenbaum. I heard tell that Mr. T had it in the works to create a conduit through nativities to deliver gifts, as a way of reaching those homes without a Christmas tree, since it's usually one or the other."

Babbo Natale and Papai Noel were on their feet quicker than it would take me to melt in hot cocoa.

"What?!" Babbo cried, turning on Kertas.

"We will have words," said Papai, removing his sunglasses.

I was shocked by the change that had come over the Santas. They'd gone from jolly and merry to lively and quick in an instant. Their cheeks were like roses, their noses like cherries, a redness clearly caused by anger.

Kertas lifted his hands defensively. "I don't think anyone would ever dream of such a thing, especially Mr. T!"

He gave me a look that asked, "Why would you say that?"

"Mr. T was always careful not to step on any toes when

it came to respecting Christmas traditions. There are so many across the world, and each is quite important to that country's inhabitants." He waved his hands. "Really, sirs, I promise, nothing of the kind was ever proposed by Mr. T. I'm not sure where Shovel got the idea."

"I'm sorry," I said, trying to defuse the situation. I'd seen what I needed to see. "You're right. It's this sloshy brain of mine. I'm sure it was someone else."

"Very well, then," said Babbo, taking a step back. "As long as you're sure." He turned to go back to his lounging, but I heard him mutter to Papai as he did so, "Perhaps it's a good thing Mr. Tannenbaum is dead, after all."

16

Trolling the Yuletide Carols

"Why would you say something like that?!" Kertas yelled at me, pulling off his red hat and whacking me with it hard enough for a bit of snow to come out of my shoulder.

"Easy now, woah," I said, sliding away from the gnome. "I just wanted to see their reaction. It's easy to assume all the Santas are off the hook, but I wanted to see if I could make them snap."

"Like peanut brittle?"

"Pretty much."

We'd been able to settle the Santas by turning the subject to food instead of gifts, and Babbo had enlightened us about the Italian tradition of the Feast of Seven Fishes and *panettone*, while Papai had told us of the *Bolo Rei*, or "King Cake," in which was hidden a bean and little gifts. If the person's slice held a gift, they could keep it, but the person who found the bean had to pay for next year's King Cake.

"Sorry," muttered Kertas, handing me some snow to fix my shoulder. "It's just that if I hear one more description of food, my belly is going to riot like children on Christmas morning."

"Are you hungry?" I asked, never having felt the sensation myself.

"More like 'hangry,'" said Kertas, replacing his hat and rubbing his stomach. "I need food."

"We could go back to Père and Baba Noël, since they offered to give you a taste of their cookies when they were finished."

"Nah, I need real food." He looked up at the moon. "The day's almost through. I'm heading home for the night. Most of the folks you hope to interview will be doing the same. Would you care to join me?"

I waved down my side. "Snowman, remember? I think I'll head back to my snowbank to mull things over."

"Nonsense, the parents would love to have you. Besides, with thirteen boys in the house, the door is always swinging open, so it's kept nice and cool."

I accepted the invitation and followed Kertas back over the snowy fields, rocks, hills, and plains to his home in the deepest, darkest part of the forest. This forest wasn't like Mr. Tannenbaum's tree farm. The darkness seemed to cling to the branches of all the trees that were in the wood, the moon's light all but hidden by the closeness of the treetops. The branches seemed to reach out to me, begging to be part of my body, and I began to wonder if it might not have been smarter to head home.

"Does Krampus live near your folks?" I asked, uneasily eyeing a particularly dark patch between two trees.

"Like I said, Krampus is nothing but a big softy," Kertas said. "Why? Has a mighty dread seized your troubled mind?"

"Yeeees," I said slowly, eyeing Kertas.

The gnome waved a hand. "That's perfectly normal. This forest naturally gives everyone a sense of dread—it's to keep all the holly jollies away. Around here, folks like to keep themselves to themselves."

"I didn't know a place like this existed at the North Pole."

"Thought it was all bright lights and candy canes and gingerbread, did you?"

"I know sometimes the frost is cruel, but yes, generally I stick to where folks prefer to dance by the light of the moon."

Kertas scoffed. "You're missing out. Only one half of Christmas is the nice kids, the other half is the naughty." He chuckled to himself and I gave him a worried glance.

"I thought you said you'd reformed and given up your candlestick-stealing days."

"I did, I did. I promise."

But something about the way the gnome was smiling made me not completely believe his words.

A soft reddish glow began to pierce the darkness before me. Although at first I wondered if Rudolph was playing hide-and-seek, I saw as we approached that it was instead a circle of bearded gnomes all seated on the ground around a campfire, just outside a wooden cabin to rival the Gingerbread Man's factory.

"Thought we'd have a stew outside tonight!" the only

woman in the bunch called out as we approached. "Good thing, too, if your snowman friend will be joining us."

The woman gave me a warm though craggy-toothed smile set in a pock-marked face that spoke of centuries of hard work. Her stringy gray hair hung about her face like wilted garlands still hanging in February as she hunched over the stewpot and served each of the gnomes.

"Sam Shovel, meet my mother, Grýla, one of the oldest trolls in Iceland."

"*The* oldest troll, Kertasníkir, me lad. And the ugliest," said a man who was easily as old, if not older, than the woman beside him. He called her "ugly" in a way that said he meant it as a compliment; I could tell straight away this was not your average family.

"And my father, Leppalúði, the grumpiest old troll in Iceland."

"A pleasure to meet you," the man said, with a raise of his cap, revealing a bald head that matched Kertas's. His grizzled beard swept the snow, though it was braided into a fantastic image of a deer in a wood.

"Does your wife braid your beard, sir? That is quite the most impressive braided image I've ever seen," I said.

"Huh? What're you talking about? This is natural." Leppalúði tried unsuccessfully to see his own beard past his enormous blotchy nose.

"My mother braids it while he's sleeping, but since there're no mirrors in the house, he has no idea," Kertas muttered to me quietly.

Grýla gave me a wink. "Have a seat, have a seat, let me introduce you to my sons."

"Can I have a scoop of stew before you begin, Ma? I'd like to eat before the Epiphany."

Grýla narrowed her eyes at her son in a way that would have turned me into a puddle in an instant, but somehow only made Kertas blush slightly.

"Sorry, Ma. It's been a long day. I've been thinking about your home-cookin' for hours."

Grýla gave another toothy grin and kissed him on the forehead, somehow making me forget they were both centuries old, reminding me instead of a mother kissing her ten-year-old son. "You do love my red cabbage stew. Let me get you some."

"Me, too, Ma."

"More, please."

"It's good, Ma. Your best."

The other brothers chorused as she set about serving up one scoop after another.

"My mother hasn't had a hot meal for herself in fifteen centuries," murmured Kertas, his green eyes as bright as the winter snow was white.

"Now, then," said Grýla, once everyone's bowls had been refilled. "You already know Kertasníkir and his penchant for stealing candles—used to have a terrible habit of eating them, poor dear, till I added a little tallow to the nightly stew."

Which made me quite happy I couldn't even try to eat it.

"And, of course, Gluggagaegir isn't here tonight because he's on duty. He likes to peer in windows and steal shiny objects like keys and coins the naughty boys and girls have left lying about. To your right is my oldest, Stekkjastaur, who starts us off every December 12th by stealing sheep from the farmers' sheds. Next to him is Hurdaskellir who stomps around slamming doors all night, keeping everyone awake. Then there's Stufur, though we all call him 'Stubby,' who likes to steal food from frying pans."

Stubby rubbed his rotund belly and declared, "Man's got to eat something other than stew!"

"Show your Ma some respect," Leppalúði said in a manner that suggested he was used to saying it often.

"What about the others?" Stubby said like a petulant boy. "Thvorusleikir, Pottaskefill, and Askasleikir all steal food from spoons, pots, and bowls." He waved toward three brothers who might have been triplets, they looked so similar. "And Skyrgamur steals skyr, Bjugnakraekir steals sausages, Gattathefur steals baked goods, and Ketkrokur steals meat."

"Especially lamb," said Ketkrokur, licking his lips before taking another large spoonful of stew.

"Even Giljagaur steals the foam from milk!"

"No more stew for you, Stubby," Grýla growled, suddenly appearing much larger than she had before. "You've gone and introduced everyone!"

Leppalúði stomped around the circle and roughly took the still-full bowl and spoon out of Stubby's hands. "That's for stealing the joy from your Ma. You know how much she loves revealing the meaning behind each of your names. Do you know how long it took her to name you all?" He shook the spoon in his son's face, flinging stew all over his reddened nose. "Never forget: she brought you into this world, and she can take you out."

"Used to be folks called Ma an ogress, said she'd boil naughty children alive if they didn't behave," Stekkjastaur, the oldest, muttered at my side.

"Anyone who'd met Ma would know that's far from true,"

said Kertas. "She's much more likely to get Jólakötturinn to do it."

"Who's Jólakötturinn?" I asked.

"Our cat," said Skyrgamur on my other side.

He and Kertas exchanged a grin.

"You say that in a way that makes me think she's not like other cats."

"*He*, and no, he's most definitely not. For one, he's bigger than our house, and he's the most blood-thirsty black cat I've ever met." Kertas glanced behind himself. "He's usually around here somewhere... Anyway, he has a taste, for some reason, for people who are not wearing at least one new piece of clothing after Christmas Eve. Not sure why. Maybe he got it from his last master, Frau Perchta."

"The Gingerbread Man's grandmother?"

"Yeah, she had this thing about punishing ladies who'd been too lazy to finish spinning their flax by Twelfth Night—January 6th, you know." Kertas shrugged. "Guess she taught him to wish the world were a better-dressed place."

"A cat that eats people, thirteen sons that slam doors and steal food, and trolls for a mother and father—there's no other family quite like yours, is there?" I tried to say it in a light-hearted manner, though I was already coming up with an excuse to leave before the night was any older.

Kertas shrugged. "We do leave candy in the shoes of the goodies, though for the baddies we leave rotting potatoes."

"That's terrible."

"It's just a bit of harmless Christmas trickery, dear," said Grýla.

"Besides, it's tradition," growled Leppalúði. "Course, we've had to cut back a bit of late. Folks don't seem to enjoy the tricks like they used to. But you can't let the naughty kids get away with gifts just like the nice ones. Why, if the bad got the same as the good, there'd be no rhyme nor reason to the world."

"Right," I said, then I stretched my branches and yawned. "Think I'll head back to my snowbank for the night. Got a lot to think through."

Kertas's eyes narrowed slightly. "Do snowmen sleep?"

"Do living snowmen dream of living snow-sheep is more the question," I said, avoiding an answer. I honestly couldn't remember if we needed sleep or not. It wasn't the sort of thing I'd written down in my notebook.

The point was, a great weariness had come over me, and I was eager to return to the lights and glowing icicles more commonly found closer to the Clauses.

And so, with another wave of my hand, I thanked Grýla for letting me meet her family, promising to meet up with Kertas in the morning next to the Claus mansion to continue our investigation.

Then I began the long slide back toward town, though I kept one eye peeled for a giant black cat.

17

Tinseling Once Again

It turns out the answer is no, snowmen don't sleep. No matter how hard I tried, and no matter how tired I felt, it seemed I was not designed for sleep. It would have made the endless night pass more quickly, but as it was, I had plenty of things to distract myself while I waited for the rest of the North Pole to wake up.

I had managed to return to my snowbank office without running into a giant black cat, an overly talkative abominable snow monster, or the creepy Krampus—whatever that guy was.

I settled in with my notebook in hand and began jotting down more extensive notes than I'd done in the past, making sure to include a list of suspects, which with two murders basically included everyone in the North Pole.

I hated seeing the list of Santas on there, so I decided I'd focus more on the other names to start.

The first on the list was also, in my opinion, the least likely suspect, but I had to include him no matter my personal feelings.

Kertas had worked as the secretary for O. Tannenbaum for too long to discount him. He knew the whereabouts of his boss at all times, and the little dirty details that had kept the business running over the years. Perhaps he knew something that he was hiding from me, some little detail that would immediately point to him as the murderer. His family was certainly from the darker corners of the North Pole, though they were more likely to be caught stealing than poisoning. It was always possible that he was following me not out of friendship or a desire to catch the guy who murdered his employer, but out of a wish to keep me close, and to ensure I never discovered the truth.

Similar facts were also true when it came to Franklin, E. Tannenbaum's secretary, though I had extreme doubts as to whether the bobble-headed turkey had the capabilities or the focus to succeed in poisoning his boss and his boss's son. Unless his birdbrained behavior was all a ploy. Perhaps he'd taken to playing up his distracted nature in order to lull everyone into a sense of security. Deep down, he could always be a psychotic who'd snapped after hearing of one too many turkey dinners...

I chuckled and shook my head at the thought. Anything was possible.

For that matter, the coroner might have done it, finding himself bored in a place where murders never occurred, and deciding it was to time to make his position a more necessary one. If there was a serial killer on the loose, there would be plenty of work for the moose.

Or maybe it was Rudolph, and he'd lied about making a deal with O. Tannenbaum to settle his debt. He'd admitted to being at the scene of the crime, perhaps he'd simply left out the part where he killed him and left him lying in the snow?

But then why kill the father, E. Tannenbaum, who—according to the reindeer—had no ties to the gambling addiction his son had acquired? Had he been silenced because he'd caught on?

What if O. Tannenbaum had been using company funds to gamble? He could have told Rudolph he wanted some extra cash off the books, but maybe he'd been lying?

Which brought me back to the girl who'd started it all, the one who'd brought me the crime in the first place.

"Oh, Sugar, Sugar," I said softly, shaking my head.

"If you start singing 'Candy Girl' you've got another think coming," grumbled Kertas, suddenly appearing at my side.

"I didn't hear you coming," I said, snapping my notebook shut and shoving it back under my fedora before he could see his own name on my list.

"Insomnia. Don't need much sleep. Probably due to the fact of growing up with a brother who thinks it's funny to run around at night slamming doors." He rubbed his neck. "Anyway, thought I'd see if you've made any progress. Figured anything out by getting those white cells working through the puzzle?"

"White cells?"

"Yeah, like Poirot's gray cells, only since you're a snowman..." He waved his hand.

"Ah," I nodded, though I had no idea who he was talking about.

"So I take it, it's time to have another little chat with a certain fairy?"

"That's what I was thinking. She'll want to hear what I've got for the case so far, and at the same time, I can ask her a few more questions now that I know more about her involvement with your boss."

"Mind if I tag along?"

"Not at all," I said, though I couldn't help thinking about the age-old phrase "keep your friends close and your enemies closer."

Kertas said he knew where to find Miss Sugar Plum, so I followed him as he led me to her tinsel factory on the other side of town. It was as far away as you could get from the peppermint farm and Tannenbaum's Christmas trees.

The building sparkled as though the entire thing was made of tinsel, the silvery gleam no doubt blinding when the sun shone directly on it during the six months of summer.

We entered the front doors, and I was pleased to find the place was cool enough that Kertas didn't even remove his hat.

"Suppose the fairies have a warmer body temp than the rest of us?" he grumbled.

"Perhaps it's from all the fluttering of their wings?" I suggested.

We approached the front desk in the lobby and waited for the pretty little fairy to put the phone down.

When she finally did, she immediately turned to me and

said in a sweet-as-marzipan voice, "Silver Leaf Fairy, what's your favorite color?"

"Um, hi, we're looking for Miss Sugar Plum?"

"Sugar's on the floor right now, can I take a message?"

"It's really important. It concerns Mr. Tannenbaum."

The fairy's silver wings fluttered and shimmered as her green eyes widened in her pale face. "Oh, dear. I did hear about what happened. So terrible. And she being so sweet on him."

"Oh? Did you know they were involved?"

"I got eyes haven't I? She lights up like a firefly whenever he's around. Or used to..."

If everyone already knew she was involved with Mr. Tannenbaum, why had she lied to me? Nothing between her and him but tinsel, she'd said. Surely she'd realized I would discover the truth eventually.

"Can we see her, please?"

"Yes, of course. Wait right there while I go get her." She began to fly away but turned back as she pulled a door open, letting in a loud chorus of voices singing, "Let's be jolly..." over the sounds of a factory at work. "Please, help yourself to some hot cocoa if you'd care to—we know not everyone enjoys the cold like we do." Then she smiled softly at Kertas with bow lips you could pin on a package before leaving and closing the door behind her.

I turned in time to catch Kertas with an awfully silly smile on his face.

"Do you...know Miss Leaf?"

Kertas's smile dropped quickly and he shuffled his feet. "Not at all," he mumbled. "Not at all."

"Kertas...if this is pertinent to the case..."

"It's not. There's nothin' between us. Fairies just have a way about them, you know. Can't help but smile when you're around one. Don't they make you feel that way?"

I shook my head.

"Must be 'cause you haven't a heart," he muttered.

The words stung. I may not have an actual heart that beats inside my chest, but I feel things just like anyone else would. I was no Tin Woodman in need of a heart. I knew I had what I needed—brains, courage, and all.

The door to the factory flung open and Miss Leaf flew in, her face paler than the marzipan I'd been thinking about earlier.

"Please—please—come quick! It's Sugar!"

Kertas and I followed at her heels, across the factory floor where all the fairies had stopped, some of them fluttering off the floor to see what was happening.

We came to a door that said "Break Room" in glittery pink writing.

Inside lay Sugar Plum, her throat wrapped in tinsel. Someone had sent Sugar into a deep and dreamless sleep as the silent stars passed by.

18

Sugar and Spice

"No one move," I said, extending my branches to either side to block anyone from entering.

Some of the fairies hovered over my shoulder, trying to peek around me.

"Not even fly-overs."

I didn't want anything contaminating the crime scene this time. No random hoof prints or piles of muddled snow to throw me off. I'd seen how much glitter a fairy dropped when flying, so I knew no one could enter the room, no matter the elevation.

I took in the scene before me, trying to imprint it all on my mind like carving an ice sculpture.

Miss Plum lay near the center of the room. The ground around her was covered in glitter, no doubt lost during the struggle. Her mouth hung open, eyes wide in terror, her wings torn and damaged beneath her. It was not the prettiest sight to see.

Near her left hand lay the broken remains of a cookie, crumbs large and small mixed with the glitter around her body. A variety of cookies, muffins, cakes, fudge, nuts, dried fruit, and more were displayed on a table in the corner, beside a cooler that no doubt held drinks to complement the treats.

"She was having a snack break. Who would attack someone while they were eating a Christmas cookie?" Kertas grumbled at my side. "It's inhuman, that's what that is."

"Murder is inhuman no matter when it's done."

"She looks like a trapped butterfly," Kertas muttered.

On that note, I knew it was time we dismissed those crowding around behind us before things escalated to panic.

I turned to Miss Leaf. "Please call the Clauses. Alert them to the situation and ask that they come immediately."

"O-of course," she whispered, her eyes never leaving her friend on the floor.

"Then call Dr. Flick." *He's got another body to keep him in business,* I couldn't help thinking to myself.

"Yes, sir," she said, then finally looked up at me, tears welling in her eyes. "She—she didn't deserve this."

"No one ever does," I said softly. I tried to give her an encouraging smile, then she turned and flew back toward the office. "Excuse us," I said to the rest, closing the door firmly so that only Kertas and I remained in the break room.

"I don't get it. I just don't get it," said Kertas, shaking his head and crossing his arms across his chest. "Why would someone do this? Why would anybody kill anyone for that matter? What's happening to this place?"

I didn't have an answer for him, but rather than having him spiral into a deeper, darker abyss, I put him to work.

"Come here and help me look for clues. Last time I wasn't at the scene, but this time I've got it all to myself."

"What are we looking for?"

I lifted my fedora and pulled out my notebook and pencil. "Anything and everything."

"That's mighty helpful," Kertas muttered, but I could tell he appreciated the distraction.

I jotted down what I'd noted on our arrival, then slid closer to Miss Plum. "My hope is that Dr. Flick will be able to tell us more details about the attack when he gets here. In the meantime, look for anything we can discover on our own. Search her pockets."

"Not much. Just some cinnamon candies, jelly beans, mint chocolates... I forgot to tell you she had a bit of a sweet tooth... There's a note!" Kertas exclaimed, excitedly pulling out a folded sheet of paper. "Your name's on it..."

He handed it to me and a whiff of cloves came with it. I unfolded the note with great hesitation.

> *Sam,*
>
> *I've been thinking through some of the things Otty told me the day before he died. I didn't have time to process them until now. I think you should know that Otty and I believed in the gift of second chances, and Christmas is the best time for offering gifts.*

I have reason to believe Otty had solved his father's murder and was planning on confronting the murderer the night he was killed. I didn't tell you because I didn't realize that was what he had planned until now. As I recall his words, I realize, that was what he was telling me.

Please come as soon as you get this. I don't want to write it all out now. Just come as soon as you can and I'll tell you everything I remember.

—Sugar

I read the note to myself before handing it to Kertas.

"Son of a nutcracker! The sap-head seriously confronted his father's murderer and expected to survive? What did he do, walk up to him and say, 'Hello, my name is Otmar Tannenbaum, you killed my father, prepare to die'?"

"Sounds to me like he didn't want revenge. He was going to give the murderer a second chance."

But Kertas wasn't listening. "Why didn't he tell me?!"

"Careful," I said, calmly trying to move the irate gnome away from the tangled remains of wings near his feet.

"Didn't he learn anything from last time?" Kertas growled at the paper.

"Poor Miss Plum." I shook my head. "The murderer must have thought she'd been told his name so she had to be...removed."

"Who is this guy? We've got to stop him, Shovel."

I beckoned for the note before Kertas accidentally tore it in half in anger.

"I'll save this in here," I said, folding it back up and placing it between the pages of my notebook to show Nick Claus when he arrived. "How about those cookies and things on the sideboard?" I pointed.

Kertas glared at the sideboard like it had killed his employer. "I could really use a candle right now," he growled as he stomped over.

I smiled and opened the fridge, taking a minute to bask in the coolness that poured out over my front. Inside was an assortment of bottled milks from whole to 2% to lactose-free to coconut and almond. There was also water, apple cider, and every color of drink from red to green, not to mention a fair collection of wines, rums, gins, and more on the side table. These fairies really liked to mix it up, apparently, even on the job.

"I guess Sugar wasn't the only one with a sweet tooth," said Kertas. "Maybe all fairies are like that."

I turned as he waved a hand over the assortment of cookies and such I'd noticed before, but also the bowls of candy, candy canes, candy corns, and syrup.

"Something tells me Miss Plum never partook of the candy canes," I said. I gave the rest of the smorgasbord a once over, then my eyes landed on something I felt I'd seen before.

I pointed to the rounded oval-shaped cookies sprinkled with powdered sugar. "Are those what I think they are?"

Kertas picked one up and smelled it. "Some sort of spiced cookie—cinnamon, I think." He took a bite.

"Wait!" I cried, then watched Kertas's face carefully for any signs of poisoning.

"It's fine. Just pistachios and honey." He nodded his bearded chin toward the fairy in the center of the floor. "She was strangled, not poisoned."

"I know, but...I just think we should be careful. Her murder has to be tied to the death of the Tannenbaums." I continued to watch the gnome's face and he continued to frown at me, but nothing more. "Anyway, was I right?"

Kertas nodded. "I'd guess these are *kahk*, the same cookies we saw a certain two Santas baking yesterday."

"Looks like they were made with the wooden press mold Baba Noël went to grab before we left."

"Wonder when they dropped these cookies off?"

They weren't the only cookies that looked familiar. I picked up one of the sugar cookies, this one shaped like a Christmas angel blowing a trumpet.

"If we're going to start pointing fingers, though, do you think this is one of Nora Claus's special cookies?"

Kertas shrugged. "Only one way to find out. Take a bite and see if you can taste anything."

"I suppose there's no way to poison a snowman..."

I tentatively bit off the trumpet, unwilling to bite off the head of the angel with a dead fairy lying behind me.

I almost melted on the spot. "Hot cocoa and marshmallows. Definitely Mrs. Claus's."

A soft tap came on the door.

"Who's that?" Kertas snapped.

"It's probably Santa Claus."

19

Sweet Hymns of Joy and Cookies

"She-she-she d-d-died quickly," Dr. Flick affirmed, which was something at least.

"So you don't think she was poisoned and then strangled?" I asked, still thinking about the scare I'd had when Kertas had eaten that cookie willy-nilly.

The coroner shook his antlers. "No, she wouldn't have been able to struggle the l-l-little she did if there'd been something in her system slowing her d-d-down."

Kertas removed his hat and placed it over his heart. "Next time I find a candle, I'll light it for her...before I eat it."

It was the thought that counted.

"This note," said Nick, holding up the paper we'd handed him, "who do you think Otmar was talking about?"

"The creature that killed his father," said Kertas, as though the answer was obvious.

"Are you sure? You really think he'd go off to confront his father's killer alone?"

"That's what it sounds like," I said.

"Have you come across any clues as to who it might have been?" Nick asked.

"Your reindeer, for one," Kertas said in a low voice very close to a growl.

"My reindeer?" Nick's eyebrows raised to his hat.

"The fact is, Nick, that Rudolph admitted he met with O. Tannenbaum the night he was murdered," I explained. "According to him, they were just meeting to come to an agreement over a sum Mr. Tannenbaum owed him. When he left, Mr. Tannenbaum was still alive."

"But we all know that reindeer can be trusted about as much as the Gingerbread Man around a basket of gumdrop buttons," Kertas grumbled.

"Careful now, that's my lead reindeer you're talking about," said Nick. He raised his hands. "I know he has his problems—gambling for one, a tendency to pridefulness another—but do you really think he'd resort to *murder*? He'd lose everything!"

"We think there's something much bigger than gambling going on here, Nick," I said, moving my pipe from one side of my mouth to the other. "Both of your head Christmas tree salesmen are dead, and now this little fairy got caught in the crossfire. Clearly the murderer thought Mr. Tannenbaum had told her who he was—"

"Or she," said Nora softly.

"Or she," I nodded in admittance. "And he or she thought it best to remove Miss Plum from the recipe before she told one of you."

"You don't think—" Nick started and then stopped.

We all waited for him to continue. Kertas not-so-sneakily grabbed another sugar cookie from the table as he did so.

"You don't think she might have asked the murderer to come to her? Hinted that she knew?"

"You mean b-b-blackmail?" Dr. Flick asked, turning from where he stood beside the sideboard, a muffin in his hoof. He shook his head. "If that's what happened here, there's no evidence of any m-m-money passing hands."

"You think the murderer would leave behind evidence?" I asked.

"If she'd held money, there'd be ink on her f-f-fingertips." He motioned with an antler toward the fairy.

"Perhaps he offered her cookies instead," Kertas suggested, waving a hand across the spread. I wondered if he paused over the *kahk* intentionally, so as to draw attention to them.

"We'll have to ask around to find out when all those sweets were delivered. I'm surprised Otmar didn't tell you before confronting the murderer," I said, removing my pipe and pointing it at Nick Claus. "You'd think he'd be smart enough to take someone with him."

Nick shook his head. "I didn't see Otmar the night or day he was murdered. I've been meeting with these Santas for the annual get-together and haven't had a chance to check on North Pole production in a couple days."

"What about you, Mrs. Claus?" I asked.

"I've been up to my elbows in flour, baking those cookies," she said, waving a hand toward the ones on the table.

"We noticed those. Do you remember when you delivered them?"

"Yes, that's why it's so sad. When I dropped them off...Sugar was still alive." Nora's shoulders slumped and tears welled in her eyes as she stared at the display of cookies. "I hope she got to enjoy at least one..."

"I'm so sorry, Mrs. Claus." I moved to put a comforting branch around her shoulders. "I have to ask, though, do you remember when that was exactly?"

"This morning. I must have just missed you and Kertas arriving. I'd only just returned to the house when we received the phone call about...her..."

"So you're saying you may have been the last person to see her alive? Did you see anyone else as you were leaving?"

"No, no one." Nora shook her head and pulled out a handkerchief, wiping her wet face. "The last time I saw her she was singing ahem..."

"Yes?"

"No, a *hymn*, as in a formal song of praise usually sung in a choral arrangement."

"Oh, a hymn." I nodded. "Out of curiosity, do you remember which one?"

"Why? Do you really think it might be important?"

"You never know what might be," said Nick.

"I think it was the one about baby Jesus."

I exchanged a look with Kertas. That narrowed it down.

"Let me think." Nora frowned in concentration. "Something about, 'risen with healing in his wings. Mild he lays his glory by, born that man no more may die, born to raise the sons of earth, born to give them second birth.'"

"Hark the Herald Angels Sing," said Kertas with a smart nod.

"She must have been thinking about second chances," I murmured.

"Poor little thing..." Nora choked. "Please, excuse me..."

She left quickly, but as the door began to close behind her I realized Miss Silver Leaf was standing on the other side, so I, too, excused myself, and followed Nora Claus out the door.

"Miss Leaf, may I have a word with you?" I asked.

She nodded and motioned back toward her desk at the front of the building. I slid along behind her, glad the fairies didn't use the floor as much as most folks, as even with the cooler temperature inside, I worried I was leaving a slipping hazard behind me. I hoped Nick, Dr. Flick, and Kertas would watch their step when they left.

As we closed the door to the factory, I was pleased to find we were alone in the foyer.

"I only had one question, really, for you," I said gently. I could tell the fairy was still somewhat in shock over the whole affair, and I didn't blame her.

Miss Leaf nodded.

"I was wondering if you could tell me who delivered all the sweets in the break room, and if so, what time?"

"Oh, those?" She brightened a little. Asking about treats was apparently a better question than another she'd been worried I'd ask. "Most of those were delivered overnight by the Gingerbread Man, though sometimes other people stop in with special items to add."

"Did any come this morning?"

"Well, Mrs. Claus brought some fresh. We'd finished off her last batch only yesterday, so that was good timing. And...those two Santas brought something new to try. They let me have a bite out here and they were absolutely delicious." Her face lit up and her wings fluttered, dropping glitter all around her.

"You must mean the *kahk*. I've heard nothing but good things about them. Did the Santas stick around at all?"

"Not really. They explained who they were and what they'd made—I can never keep track of all the Santas. They also brought some fancy bread. It all looked and smelled quite wonderful." Her smile drooped. "You don't think—I mean, I thought—"

"No, no, the coroner says she wasn't killed by cookies. Don't you worry. I'm just trying to piece together who's been here, other than fairies."

"There's no way another fairy did that," said Miss Leaf adamantly. Then she cocked her head. "For one thing, I don't think any of us would have the strength to kill a fellow fairy."

"You mean physically?"

She nodded.

I echoed her nod.

"Oh, and Mrs. Cane," she said suddenly, "came by with some candy canes, which we all love...except for...Sugar..."

At that moment, we were joined by Kertas. *Just in time*, I thought. Time to return to the candy cane fields for a little chat with Mrs. Cane.

20

O'er the Fields We Go

"Nick said he'd help Dr. Flick get Sugar back to the morgue, though the fairies might have something to say about that."

"You think they won't allow it?" I asked over the *crunch, crunch, crunch* of Kertas stomping through the snow beside me.

"I'm pretty sure they have their own burial rituals that are a little different from most."

"I bet Dr. Flick will release the body quickly. Like he said, she was strangled. Period."

Kertas nodded in agreement.

"What I still don't get is why Miss Plum told me there was nothing between her and Mr. Tannenbaum except their business relationship? Why would she lie to me about something I'd obviously find out sooner or later? After all, it's not like you tried to keep it a secret from me."

"Because I could see you were on the case."

"But I was on the case because she put me on it. I might not have even considered investigating if she hadn't come into my office the morning I woke up."

"They *were* trying keeping their relationship a secret," Kertas said with a shrug. "Maybe she just didn't want to cloud your judgement."

"Why?"

"Why what?"

"Why keep their relationship a secret?" I pressed. "There's nothing wrong with a fairy and a man being in a relationship. If that were true, Peter Pan would have been brought in for questioning centuries ago."

"How on earth do you know Peter?" Kertas asked. "He hasn't traveled this far north in...ever, as far as I know."

I moved my pipe from one side of my mouth to the other. "You know...I don't know."

"Besides, I don't think Peter and Tink's relationship is quite the same. And Mr. T and Sugar were unique, as well, given they weren't just any old man and fairy. They were the head of the North Pole Christmas Tree Emporium and one of the lead sales fairies of the North Pole Tinsel Factory."

"Romeo and Juliet?"

"More like Mr. T didn't want his competitors to get it into their heads that his relationship with Sugar had any impact on his support of other suppliers."

"Like candy canes?" I asked as we neared the fields I'd visited the morning before.

"Precisely."

This time I couldn't hear the roar of the crooker, but I could see it parked way out on the top of a hill devoid of canes, work lights around it. Someone's feet stuck out from underneath.

I exchanged glances with Kertas and then the two of us rushed across the fields like shoppers on Black Friday.

Somehow, the gnome beat me to it, reaching down a few inches to yank on the feet.

"Ow!" the someone cried, a head banging the under-workings of the crooker with a clang that made my own head hurt. "Field and fountain! What in the silver bells?!"

Out slid a young woman who looked enough like Mrs. Cane for me to realize it was her daughter, CanDee, her short, cropped hair dyed red with white streaks in it, the opposite of her mother's. She wore overalls spattered with dark spots, which I hoped was oil rather than blood.

"What's the meaning of this?" she cried, her nose still slightly plugged from the cold her mother had mentioned.

"Sorry, CanDee, we thought you were in trouble," Kertas said in a low, embarrassed tone, removing his hat to wipe his head. "I'm so glad you weren't dead."

"Dead?" CanDee pushed herself up on her elbows, giving her forehead a rub where she'd conked it good and proper. "I ain't no Little Nell. I'm just trying to fix this hunk-o-junk so I can get back to work." She punched the side of the crooker, then shook her hand, realizing she'd done nothing more than hurt another body part. "Of course it would break down two days before Christmas."

"Anything we can do?" I asked, knowing full well there wasn't. I was pretty sure neither of us knew the first thing about mechanics.

"Yeah, don't tell Dad." CanDee blew messily into a handkerchief before she picked up a wrench from a pile of tools including a hammer and lots of tacks, and pointed it at us with a glare. "I can fix it myself."

"We were actually looking for your mother," I said.

"She's over at the barn," CanDee said with a sniff, waving in the general direction before sliding back under the crooker.

Apparently, our conversation was over.

Kertas and I slid along in the direction CanDee Cane had indicated, eventually coming to a large barn from which emanated the sweet smell of peppermint in an almost overwhelming manner.

"I wonder why the smell is stronger here than in the fields."

"Perhaps the peppermint gets stronger after they're picked?" Kertas suggested.

"Are we near the area where you found him?" I eyed the middle distance, trying to tell if just beyond those canes stood a grove of trees wherein murder had occurred.

"I'd guess so," said Kertas quietly. "Let's get this over with. I keep half-expecting to round another corner only to find another body." He shivered slightly.

I pitied him. There was a good reason we'd both jumped to the conclusion of yet another murder when we'd first seen CanDee. In the past two days, Kertas had come across two dead bodies. No wonder the guy needed a candle.

I knew then and there what I was getting him for Christmas.

"Hey there, snowman," called Mrs. Cane with a friendly

wave, stepping out from behind a crate of candy canes with a clipboard in hand as we entered the barn. "I see you found the Tannenbaum establishment, or what's left of it." She gave Kertas a nod. "Did you catch him yet?"

"Who?" I asked, feigning ignorance.

"The murderer of my cohort in crime."

I raised my twig eyebrows.

Mrs. Cane raised her hands, the clipboard going with them. "Mr. Tannenbaum, of course. I was only joking. Don't look so serious. What? Did something else happen?"

"You might say that," growled Kertas, back to his usual grumpy old self. "You know the fairy Sugar Plum?"

"Frosty here knows I do," Mrs. Cane said curtly.

"She's dead," I said, just as curtly, hoping for a reaction.

I got one, maybe even the one I'd been expecting.

"Ah, I take it she won't be winging her flight over all the earth anymore? Good thing, I was getting tired of seeing her little light shining over my fields where it wasn't wanted."

"What do you mean?"

"I mean little Miss Tinsel had gotten it into her head to fly over our candy cane fields on her way to Mr. Tannenbaum's, even though our fields are covered by a strict no-fly zone."

"Did you report her?"

"To who? If you haven't noticed, there aren't any cops up here."

I blinked. I actually hadn't really thought about it yet, but come to think of it, she was right. When we'd discovered the body of Miss Plum, the first people I'd called had been the doc and Nick Claus.

"I suppose that makes Mr. Claus the chief of police?"

"In a way," she agreed.

"So...did you tell him?"

Mrs. Cane shook her head. "Nah. It's irritating, especially when she gets glitter all over the canes in her flight path, but it's not like she's killing them off—though I think that was her intention." Mrs. Cane leaned in close and lowered her voice. "Honestly, she was doing me a favor. The glitter canes have been a huge success!" She raised her brows and nodded happily.

"I see. So actually, you didn't mind?"

"It's the principle of the thing. When I'm out watching over my fields by night I didn't like seeing someone disobeying clearly posted signs."

"Oh? So there are signs? She knew it was against the rules?"

"Of course! She was doing it to spite me. She was always doing things like that."

"You certainly seem to have a strong dislike for her," Kertas grumbled.

"Well, I'm no Scrooge. But I'm also no saint. Sure I 'disliked' her—she was my competition."

"There's only one certain way to remove an obstacle like that," I murmured.

Mrs. Cane crossed her arms. "Why would I kill her? I'm happily married. Got the family business. Like I said, the only reason I didn't get on with her was because we were competitors."

"Only for Christmas trees? Or the man behind them, as well?"

Mrs. Cane straightened. "I don't like what you're insinuating Mr. Frosty."

"It's Shovel, ma'am. Sam Shovel."

"Well, I ain't no raspberry tart, if that's what you're implying. The Tannenbaums and Canes have been working together for centuries—centuries! Why would I up and murder them? What good would that do anybody?"

"I didn't say anything about the Tannenbaum murders..."

Mrs. Cane set down her clipboard and pulled her handkerchief from her overall pocket to wipe her brow, her moves slow and methodical. "The point is, I have no 'motive'—isn't that the word you detectives use—for killing anybody, either the fairy or the Tannenbaums."

"Perhaps I haven't landed on it yet, but you certainly had opportunity."

Mrs. Cane scoffed. "What opportunity? I've been out here working the candy cane fields every day from moon-up to moon-down since last New Year's Day."

"I found Mr. T in that corner of his Christmas tree lot," Kertas said, pointing out the door of the barn toward the grove just visible over the canes.

Mrs. Cane's face went as pale as an un-reddened candy cane. "*That* corner?"

"Yes," I confirmed. "That corner. Mind telling me what's so special about that corner?"

Mrs. Cane's eyes darted to my coal ones and then down at the ground. "No reason. No reason at all."

21

A Crooked Hoss

"Come now, Mrs. Cane, I need you to tell me. This is a murder investigation. When you hold back secrets, it makes you look guilty."

"I'm not guilty of anything!" she proclaimed, picking up her clipboard again.

"Then tell me what's so special about that corner of the Christmas tree lot. It just so happens to be quite close to your fields and—"

"I met with him that night," Mrs. Cane blurted, then seemed to instantly regret it, her face crumpling as she lifted her clipboard to hide behind it.

But it was too late.

"You, too?" Kertas asked.

She lowered the clipboard. "Me, 'too'? Who else met with him?"

"Never mind that," I said, giving Kertas a look. It was no business of Mrs. Cane's whether we had other suspects on the line. "Why did you meet with Mr. Tannenbaum the night of his murder?"

"We had a...an understanding."

"What sort of understanding?"

"It wasn't anything illegal."

Said the Grinch. "Then what was it?" I asked aloud.

Mrs. Cane sighed and rubbed her temple, sagging onto a bale of hay beside the rows of crated candy canes. "As long as candy canes remained the top decoration on Christmas trees," she mumbled, "more than candles or tinsel or pickles or apples or anything like that, I promised to give him a percentage of sales."

"How much?"

"Not much." She lowered her voice even more. "Only two percent."

My eyes widened. Two percent of millions of sales was still quite a bit.

I whistled.

"It wasn't much," she insisted. "Just a little...incentive...to keep him honest."

"Honest?!" Kertas yelled, making us both jump. "What's honest about that? You were bribing him to keep you in business."

Mrs. Cane scoffed and rolled her eyes. "I didn't need him to keep us in business. Candy canes aren't going anywhere. I just wanted to ensure he wouldn't start pushing tinsel over candy canes just because he had a little Feast of Stephen on the side. It's not personal. It's business."

"It's practically blackmail."

"That sounds an awful lot like motive to me," muttered Kertas.

I agreed.

"He didn't have to take it. He could've turned me down. Instead he agreed to meet me every once in awhile to discuss sales and transfer money from my account to his."

"Did your husband know about this?" I asked.

Mrs. Cane scoffed again. I was getting really tired of that sound. "It was Spear's idea."

Spear O'Mint Cane: the head of the candy cane empire for as long as I could remember. Probably went back as far as the Tannenbaums.

"How long had this little arrangement been going on?"

"About two months after we learned Otmar had started dating little Miss Tinsel."

"Only two months? You got worried that quickly?"

Mrs. Cane shrugged. "It was clear it had been going on far longer than that. We weren't sure how serious things were so we thought it best to strike up an arrangement. Even if—more like when—he broke up with her, it wasn't a bad thing to offer a bit of encouragement to keep ourselves on top."

"When did you meet with him that night?"

"I'm not sure. Late."

"Did you see anyone else?"

"Nope. Not a soul."

"Any...footprints or hoof prints?"

Mrs. Cane narrowed her eyes. "Not that I noticed."

"Only you went? Mr. Cane didn't join you? Or CanDee?"

"Nope, just me. I'm in charge of finances, so it was my job and mine alone, even though Mr. Cane was aware of it."

"What about CanDee?"

"She's been sick in bed, like I told you." Mrs. Cane smiled slightly. "If she'd been anywhere nearby, I would have heard her sneezing, or at least sniffling."

I nodded. It all seemed on the up and up. But I knew I was missing something.

"Did you ever meet Mr. Tannenbaum in his office?"

"Never, we always met at that place where our two fields parallel. It was a private transaction—we didn't want anyone snooping around and getting the wrong idea."

Nothing like a clandestine meeting to *not* give people the wrong idea.

"So I couldn't have poisoned him."

"How'd you know he was poisoned?" Kertas growled, beating me to the question.

Mrs. Cane waved her hand. "Everyone knows. It's not like the North Pole is a big place. And murder is a bit strange to be happening here, so naturally it's on everyone's tongue, more common than spiced cookies for once."

"So you know..."

"I know Otmar died of soap poisoning in his eggnog, yes," she said.

"We actually don't know for sure if it was in his eggnog," I pointed out. "Kertas cleaned the cup before we could have it tested."

If I'd had a lip to bite, I would have bitten it. I shouldn't have said that in front of a suspect.

"Oh really?" Mrs. Cane raised a brow.

I turned to Kertas. "May I speak with you privately?"

He followed me outside the barn a little ways where I lowered my voice for privacy's sake.

"I take it you had no idea he had this little arrangement with the Canes?" I asked.

The gnome shook his head. "Mr. T must have kept it off the books."

"I'm thinking that's where he was getting the gambling money." I shook my head. "I don't get it. Why, if he was getting a small percentage of a couple million, did he need more money from gambling?"

"Maybe it just started as a hobby, something fun to do," suggested Kertas, "and Rudolph took the reindeer by the horns and made Mr. T lose so much he was actually down a couple million, instead of up."

"Was there anyone he didn't meet with that night?"

"Sugar," said Kertas sadly.

I nodded slowly. We knew for certain both Rudolph and Mrs. Cane had met with Mr. Tannenbaum the night of his murder. But only Mrs. Cane had also been seen at the tinsel factory.

The problem was, both of them had willingly admitted to it, while adamantly denying they could have been the murderer. Would the murderer really be so open about his or her movements? Maybe to lull me into a false sense of security? Or was I completely off the scent? Lost amidst the peppermint and spice?

Kertas and I returned to the barn, though I was still considering what question to ask next.

"My turn," said Mrs. Cane as we entered, standing and setting down her clipboard. "May I speak with you? Just you, Frost—I mean, Shovel."

I raised my eyebrows and glanced at Kertas. "Sure."

Mrs. Cane and I left the barn, going to stand about where Kertas and I had just been. I couldn't help glancing down to check that her hands were empty. I hadn't forgotten about that brick that came soaring out of nowhere and through my middle when Kertas and I had first visited the scene of the crime yesterday.

The candy cane farmer rubbed her hands together, then placed them in her overall pockets, as though that was the only way to get them to stop moving. "Shovel, I have to ask, why are you so sure you don't have the culprit already in hand?"

I frowned. "What do you mean?"

"I mean..." Mrs. Cane checked around us and then leaned in close. "Kertas. The secretary. Are you keeping him close because you're keeping an eye on him?"

"No...," I said slowly. "He's helping me solve the case. He wants to catch the murderer of his employer as bad as I do."

"Does he?" Mrs. Cane straightened.

"What are you implying, Mrs. Cane?"

"He's the one who found his boss dead—opportunity. You just told me that he cleaned the cup holding Mr. Tannenbaum's eggnog, most likely to hide the suspicious nature of what was inside—means and opportunity again." She counted off on her fingers. "And you know who's going to take over the

Christmas tree industry with no more Tannenbaums in line to succeed?"

I moved my pipe from one side of my mouth to the other. I'd been really trying to avoid this very thought.

"Kertas."

22

Light a Candle

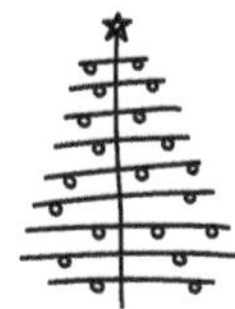

"You look like a kid who's found rotten potato peelings in his shoe on Christmas morning," said Kertas.

I took in the gnome at my side. I just couldn't believe it. I knew all the points laid out against him, but I still couldn't believe it. Besides, I owed him an apology for sharing the bit about the eggnog cup in front of Mrs. Cane.

"I'm sorry. I didn't mean to make it sound like you had something to do with... I know you didn't."

"Thanks, Shovel. Means a lot to hear you say that."

Crunch, crunch, slide, slide.

"My own family thinks I did it."

"Really?"

"Yeah. I think they think it was a joke gone horribly wrong, so they're keeping mum about it, as a family should do."

I straightened my scarf, more to give my hands something to do before I asked a rather difficult question.

"Kertas, I have to ask, *are* you inheriting the Tannenbaum company?"

The gnome blew out his cheeks and mumbled something. "Yes, apparently I am."

I nodded slowly. "Did something change since yesterday morning? I think you told me you weren't the next in line when I first met you."

"Yeah. I met with the lawyers this morning, before coming to grab you. Messrs. Present, Past, and Future of G.H.O.S.T., Limited. I didn't know the silly man had left me everything..."

I glanced at Kertas. He was crying.

"He...he said...in the will...that it was because...from the very beginning...candles were what adorned the Christmas tree...so who better to take over..." The gnome let out a quiet sob.

I stopped and put a branch around his shoulders. To my surprise, he turned into me and pressed his face into my snow.

"There, there," I said softly, unsure what else to say.

Sometimes the best thing is to not say anything at all.

A few minutes later, we were back on the path, though I wasn't really sure where we were headed. We'd left behind the candy cane fields and seemed to be meandering back along the same road I'd first taken, past The Gingerbread House, from which the sweet spicy smells of freshly baked cookies were emanating, around Milky Lake toward the gumdrop road, which would eventually dead-end at Tannenbaum's Christmas Tree Farm.

"I didn't want to make things worse in there," I said, "but I think it's important to note that Ernst Tannenbaum didn't have mistletoe in his eggnog, but rather in his tea, so it's not necessarily a matter of eggnog."

"I suppose it could've been in something he ate with the tea, just like it could have been something Mr. T ate with his eggnog."

"That doesn't narrow it down, unless Mr. Tannenbaum regularly ate something every night with his eggnog?"

"Sorry, no," said Kertas. "We always kept a fresh platter in the office, a lot like at the tinsel factory. Everything from cookies to fudge was on hand at all times."

"As I recall, the ingredients the coroner found in his belly make up practically every sweet invented."

"And who's to say Mr. T didn't grab multiple things at once? Everyone's always eating something this time of year."

Except for me, I thought, that glorious taste of hot cocoa and marshmallows coming back to me from the sugar cookies of Mrs. Claus's I'd tasted.

"If we go based on treats, at least we can throw out the two Noëls," said Kertas. "They didn't make their *kahk* until yesterday, after Mr. T was dead."

"Père Noël and Baba Noël were still in town, though," I pointed out, "and could have just as easily whipped up a batch of something less suspicious, something that wouldn't immediately point the finger at them. You can make a lot more than *kahk* with those ingredients they had out."

"Which, if they're really the murderers, would make sense. Whoever this guy is, he's smart."

I nodded in agreement.

Just then, I noticed who was approaching us down the road. I lifted a branch to wave.

"Hello again!" the Gingerbread Man called in response, his licorice smile widening beneath his candy eyes.

"How's your day going, Merry?" Kertas asked, giving the cookie a friendly handshake.

"Good, good. Just dropped off the day's cookies at your offices." He held up a large empty basket with red and green ribbons woven through the braided rattan. "I figured even if Mr. Tannenbaum is no longer with us, I shouldn't skimp on spreading a little Christmas cheer to the others working up to the last stroke of midnight on Christmas Eve."

"And longer. The workdays don't really slow down for us until the end of January. That's when we give everyone a much needed break," said Kertas.

"Same, same," said Merry. "A cookie's work is never truly finished, though. Every day is fit for a cookie!"

"Well said." Kertas practically huzzah-ed. "You wouldn't happen to have—"

"Of course, my good gnome. I always keep a few extra on hand." Merry smiled and searched in his satchel briefly before pulling out an iced gingerbread man that looked a lot like himself.

"You're the reason those tiny tots have eyes all aglow this time of year," Kertas declared, happily taking a large bite.

Much to my chagrin, he'd snapped the head right off the cookie, and I noticed Merry wince just slightly at the sight. I wondered if he remembered what it had been like to be a man before he became all cookie.

"Where are you off to next?" I asked.

"Back to the Nutcracker Suites. Some of the Santas still in town have placed a large order for some of their more traditional cookies."

"Like *kahk*?"

"Seems to me the Noëls have those ones well in hand. Have you tried them yet? I had Baba Noël write down his recipe for me. They were quite excellent!"

"I had the pleasure," said Kertas, "but of course, Shovel here hasn't."

"Too bad. Perhaps Nora Claus could whip up something you could taste. Word around town is, even snowmen can taste her magical sugar cookies." Merry gave me a wink.

"That's true."

"Unfortunately, she refuses to pass along her recipe. Says with great power comes great responsibility, and I suppose she's right." The cookie shrugged. "If I had the ability to make cookies that always tasted perfect for everyone, well, the world would be a much happier place, don't you think? Of course, gingerbread itself is more than a cookie. It can be used for everything from biscotti to building houses." Merry waved toward his own factory.

"Seems you're already spreading joy everywhere you go," I said, motioning toward his empty basket.

"Indeed. What's Christmas without a spiced cookie? The very smell of ginger, cinnamon, cardamom, nutmeg, cloves, all those spices evoke Christmas."

It was funny how everyone seemed to think their element of Christmas was the most important. Miss Plum had been all for tinsel, the Canes voted for peppermint, the reindeer had wanted more carrots involved, Merry said it came down to cookies and spice, and Mr. Tannenbaum had no doubt been convinced that the smell of pine was the crucial essence of Christmas.

I wondered if they didn't all have it wrong. It seemed to me that Christmas wasn't about one thing or another, it was about all of them together.

But this year, something was fracturing at the North Pole. People were pointing fingers at each other, worrying about who was the biggest, most important. I worried that if I didn't act quickly, it was going to start seeping out across the world, infecting not just the North Pole's inhabitants but everyone.

"If everyone's doing so well," grumbled Kertas, "why did someone feel they had to murder Mr. T?"

Merry shook his head sadly. "If I were you, I'd check out an industry that's failing. One that maybe felt pressure from the Christmas tree sales."

"Like who?"

"What's a Christmas tradition you haven't seen in awhile?"

I mulled this over in my mind, though what with the Gingerbread Man's naturally spice-filled aroma and one thing and another, my brain was starting to feel more like mulled wine.

Kertas snapped his fingers. "How about the Nutcracker?"

23

The Nutcracker Suites

"I had no idea sales were this bad," Kertas said with a shake of his head.

After Kertas had suggested speaking to the Nutcracker, Merry had said he'd come with us if we could just swing by The Gingerbread House so he could pick up some more cookies for delivery.

"I thought you said you were headed to the Nutcracker Suites?" I'd asked. "Aren't we more likely to find the Nutcracker at the factory?"

It was then Merry had let us in on just how bad things had gotten.

When we'd visited the Nutcracker Suites before, we'd caught

the Noëls in active baking mode in the outdoor kitchens, so I'd assumed the rest of the hotel was as decoratively appointed. And I wasn't wrong. This was a high-class hotel, probably the highest in the North Pole, which had plenty to offer on the bed and breakfast front, since one of our main industries was tourism.

According to the plaque outside, the designer of the hotel had based it on his favorites from around the globe, so visitors had the option of staying in wings inspired by the Taj Mahal or Neuschwanstein Castle or ice palaces to rival Andersen's Snow Queen's.

Because they catered to all individuals, their front desk was thoughtfully set up as half inside and half outside, so that folks like myself could slide right up without worrying about melting upon entrance.

This also meant we could see who was currently working as concierge.

"Welcome to the Nutcracker Suites, where your dreams will include your choice of dancing sugar plums, waltzing flowers, or spinning chocolates from your preferred country." The drone of the voice was in opposition to the smile plastered across his face, his movements as wooden and mechanical as a tin soldier.

"Nuss Knacker himself is working the front desk?" Kertas asked Merry in a low voice.

The Gingerbread Man nodded. "Time was, the Nutcracker was one of the top sales people in the North Pole. He's still got a factory in town, it's just not where the main income is coming from these days."

"But...running his own hotel?" Kertas shook his head. "Sugared pecans, how the mighty have fallen!"

"I think he actually enjoys it, although it's difficult to know for sure because his smile is painted on."

Since the nutcracker's mustache and eyebrows had been painted on as well, the only physical indication that Mr. Knacker was not as happy as he might seem was the way his black beard and sideburns drooped around his shining white teeth.

"Is the pool open?" asked the female half of the penguin couple currently checking in.

"The pool is under the gym floor and opens every day from one a.m. to three a.m. and from nine p.m. to eleven p.m.... Unless some child has dropped a chocolate Santa, in which case I wouldn't swim in it with a thirty-nine-and-a-half-foot pole."

"That doesn't make sense," said the male penguin. "How would you swim with a pole that long?"

"Especially when the pool is only forty feet long," said Mr. Knacker.

The penguins exchanged a glance.

"I see... Well, what temperature is our room set at?" the male asked. "My wife and I are African Black-Footed Penguins, so we actually prefer between 5 and 20 degrees Celsius."

"What is that in Fahrenheit?" Mr. Knacker asked.

"I'm not sure." The male glanced about.

"Roughly 42 to 68 degrees Fahrenheit," Merry answered from behind them.

The penguins turned around.

"Conversions are pretty standard in my line of work."

Merry smiled and lifted his basket. “Baking,” he said, offering the penguins each a fish-shaped cookie.

They cocked their heads in a genial manner and took them before turning back to Mr. Knacker, who had clearly forgotten they’d just asked a question.

“Please do not hesitate to ask for anything you require during your stay. Have a nice day.” With a turn of his wooden hand, he waved the penguin couple to an ice escalator, beyond which I could see the spires of an ice castle.

The penguins shrugged to one another and waddled off with their suitcases and cookies in each flipper.

Nuss Knacker turned back to us. “Welcome to the Nutcracker Suites, where your dreams—oh, right, more cookies.”

“Of course! This time of year, you can’t have enough cookies on offer.”

The Nutcracker’s eyelids lowered. “Used to be nuts were what folks couldn’t get enough of...but times change. Cookies today, most likely fudge tomorrow.”

“Oh, fudge! I love fudge!” said Merry, surprising us all.

“I figured you for a cookie man,” I said.

“I love all sweets. Anything that puts a smile on folks’ faces.” The corners of Merry’s licorice mouth lifted at this. “But I’d say you’re wrong, Nuss. Folks are leaning toward the healthy foods these days: nuts and apples are back on the rise. I bet your factory will be pumping again soon enough. Everything has its season. From what I hear, nutcrackers are selling just fine in Germany, and in German households across the world, and anytime someone puts on that ballet there’s an upswing in sales. I still get requests for nutcracker-shaped cookies all the time.” He held an example aloft from his basket, the cookie painted to match Mr. Knacker's blue and red suit. Merry's icing decorators had even captured the Nutcracker's smile.

The man himself studied the cookie. "I suppose you're right. Folks do love the ballet...unless the lead dancer twists her ankle, or the prince can't perform perfect *fouettés* or *pas de bourrees* or—"

"Well, guess I better be off," interrupted Merry happily. "Those platters won't refill themselves! But first, one more for the road?" he asked Kertas, who happily helped himself to a gingerbread cookie shaped and iced like a Santa hat.

"Thanks," he said, as we waved to Merry. Kertas slipped the cookie under his real Santa hat, saving it for later.

"Welcome to the Nutcracker Suites, where your dreams will include—"

"Nuss, it's me, Kertas. This is Sam Shovel."

"We have some lovely iced rooms, unless the air-conditioner's broken, in which case I don't suppose you'd be very comfortable." He eyed my snowballs. "Unless you're trying to slim down."

"Whoever heard of a skinny snowman?" Kertas grumbled, and I appreciated the sentiment.

"Not today," I said to Mr. Knacker. "We've got a few questions for you."

"Yes, I know about the rats in the rooms. They're actually large mice. It can't be helped." Mr. Knacker sighed. "I had to let the Mouse King have his pick of rooms. He is co-owner after all. So don't go throwing any shoes at them or I'll hear about it."

"It's not about that," I said. "There's been another murder."

The Nutcracker sighed. "I'll call the janitor." He reached for the phone.

"No, no, not here," said Kertas, but it was too late.

It was like talking to a toy train with a one-track mind.

"Please come to the front desk when you're able, unless you're still gluing that loose newell post, or cleaning up after the fried cat under the armchair in the lobby, or fixing the furnace, or..." After listing at least twenty-five more things, he finally hung up the phone and turned his smile back on us.

"You didn't need to do that," I said. "The murder didn't happen here. Miss Plum died at the tinsel factory."

"Miss Plum?" For the first time, some semblance of a reaction crossed the painted face, the Nutcracker's eyes widening in surprise, his cheeks reddening to a deeper shade.

"Did you know Miss Plum?" I asked.

"She was my girlfriend..."

I turned to Kertas to ask if he'd known the fairy had been seeing someone in addition to Mr. Tannenbaum, but then Mr. Knacker continued: "Until she left me for someone less..."

Gloomy, negative, milk-glass-half-empty, I wanted to say.

"...me," the Nutcracker finished.

I wondered if what the guy really needed was a hug.

"When did things end between you?" Kertas asked.

"A long time ago. Back when I was...popular."

"What did I tell you about being dismal with the guests?" a familiar voice said behind us.

We turned to find the janitor had joined us.

"Ma?" said Kertas, his voice lifting from its usual growl for once. "What are you doing here?"

"Oh, hello, dear," Grýla said, parking her cleaning mobile.

"Don't let old Knacker fool you. This hotel is making money hand over fist. He just likes to put a realistic touch on things. It's why I came to work for him. He's one of the few people who doesn't try to fake it during the holidays."

"And you're one of the few people who doesn't mind constantly cleaning up after others."

"Thirteen kids will do that to you," Grýla said with a smile, ruffling her son's hat.

"Hey!" he shouted, pulling off his Santa hat and dumping out the crumbly remains of his gingerbread cookie. "I was saving that!"

"Well, I'm not cleaning those crumbs," said Grýla, crossing her arms.

"You're as bad as Frau Perchta," Kertas mumbled under his breath, but not low enough.

Grýla clapped him on the head.

"Ow!"

"Don't ever let me hear you comparing me to that old crone. This place was spotless, I tell you, *spotless* when she died. It's a good thing I came along to continue her work." Grýla handed Kertas a broom and dustpan. "That's your mess, young man, so you better clean that up this instant."

To my astonishment, Kertas knelt immediately and began sweeping.

I supposed I should be grateful I didn't have a mother.

"Mr. Knacker," Grýla turned to her boss, "I checked every one of those imported Italian twinkle lights and not one of them is broken."

"All twenty-five thousand?"

"Yes, all two hundred fifty strands, one hundred bulbs per strand. It must be an internal electrical issue."

"Did you try turning them off and on again?"

"Yes. And Room 1983 needs glue."

"What for?"

"Something about a broken leg or a broken lamp, or maybe both."

"We're out of glue."

Grýla leaned over the desk and whispered forcefully, "You used up all the glue on purpose, then, because we had a full bottle yesterday when I fixed that newel post."

"It's still wobbly."

"Then give me a chainsaw and I'll fix it proper."

24

Peace on Earth

As soon as Kertas finished cleaning up his crumbs, we excused ourselves and left the hotel, only to walk smack into another Santa.

"*Ní hǎo*," Sheng Dan Lao Ren said with a nod of his head. He took a crunchy bite out of his apple, his lips and chin outlined by his white beard. "Ooo, a juicy one," he said with a laugh, wiping his wet fingers on his embroidered hanfu covered in long, thin dragons encircling Christmas trees and...saxophones? "Would you like one?" he reached into his pocket and offered it to us.

"I'm afraid I can't eat," I said with a smile.

"No, no, friend, I meant would you like it for your nose."

He waved toward my carrot nose. "This is a Peace Apple, a Christmas gift from me to you. A few days early, yes, but it is the North Pole, after all, and here every day is Christmas, no?"

"It always feels that way to me," I agreed, since I was one of the few people in the world who only lived for the twelve days of Christmas.

"'Looks like any other apple,' said Snow White to the Witch," Kertas grumbled at my side. "What makes your apple so special, if I might ask? I'm more for cookies than fruit, you see." He wrinkled his nose like he really did believe all fruit was poisoned.

Sheng Dan Lao Ren laughed and threw the apple in the air, nearly hitting one of the hanging paper lanterns along the pathway. "I will take a bite out of it if you would like. An apple a day makes this Santa feel the joy of Christmas, you know." His eyes sparkled. "But to answer your question, this apple, *ping guo*, is a Peace Apple because it is gifted on Christmas Eve, *ping'an ye*, or 'peaceful night,' and the two words sound quite similar, yes? So we like to say that eating an apple on Christmas Eve will bring you peace and safety in the year to come."

"I take it you must live in an orchard with your dragons?" I asked.

The Chinese Santa looked down at his hanfu and the embroidery *moved*, the dragons swirling around the trees, the saxophones dancing as a soft lilt of music filled the air. Living at the North Pole should make me less impressed by magic, but I tell you, it never gets old.

"You are half right. Our home contains one of the largest orchards in the world, but I am afraid the time of dragons has passed. It is only me and my sisters who live there now."

Kertas's eyes lit up. "How many sisters do you have?"

"I am afraid I lost count several hundred years ago."

Kertas whistled. "Did any travel with you here?" He looked around like he expected to see a young lady hiding behind one of the trees.

"Not this year." Sheng's eyes twinkled merrily. "But if you are interested, you are welcome to visit anytime. My sisters would love to meet you. Perhaps next year when Nick travels through to check on the S-ANTA you could tag along." Sheng's face fell as he added, "I was sorry to hear about the demise of Otmar. He was a kind soul. Whenever he visited, we would jam together."

"Jam?" I asked.

"Yes, Otmar had quite the talent for the trumpet, and with my sax, along with some of my sisters, we had a full band to repeat the sounding joy sweetly through the night."

"Your sisters play instruments?" Kertas asked.

"Mr. Tannenbaum played trumpet?" I asked at the same time.

"Mr. T's talent with the trumpet was enough to make anyone bring him some figgy pudding just so he'd leave, but yeah, he played," Kertas said.

"Oh, I would not say that!" Sheng laughed. "Otmar was gifted! His only problem was knowing when to call it a night!" He laughed again at the memory. "There were no silent nights with him... I will miss him. Will you continue his work?"

"Yeah," said Kertas softly.

Sheng placed the apple he'd been eating back in the folds of his hanfu, then reached out and put one hand on the gnome's shoulder while proffering a fresh apple. "*Shèng dàn jié kuài lè.*"

Kertas took the apple with a muttered thank you, and I could tell he was touched, even if he was trying not to let on.

"So in China you use Christmas trees?" I asked, changing the subject while Kertas tucked his apple up under his hat. At least it couldn't be crushed into crumbs.

"Indeed we do. We call them 'Trees of Light' because we hang paper lanterns on them that glow like stars with royal beauty. There are lanterns everywhere—inside and outside—a festival of colors to make the season bright. At night the streets shine so it is difficult to believe the sun has set." He looked about at the strands of lights and lanterns hanging above our heads. "Much like here, in fact."

"So the S-ANTA was a simple addition to your traditions?"

"Of course, though I often discussed the idea with Otmar of stretching beyond trees to somehow incorporate the use of lanterns or strings of lights, since it seemed to me that would expand the effective reach of the S-ANTA system."

"That's a good point," said Kertas, rubbing his chin. "Everyone uses lights this time of year, even those on the sunny side of the world."

"Even in Russia," said a deep voice from behind us.

Coming along the path was Ded Moroz and his gorgeous granddaughter, Snegurka, their robes still carrying a natural luminescence all their own.

"In our country, the children make a circle around the Christmas tree and call for us, and when we appear, the lights on the tree light up."

"As well as the star on the top," Snegurka added, pointing to the half-moon on her own head and then to the gibbous one in the sky above us, surrounded by stars that sparkled nearly as much as the ones on her dress.

"You're still here as well? I thought most of the Santas would have left by now," I said, though I was pleased to see Snegurka and her twin braids again. "I'm Sam. I believe I saw you earlier at the Santa meeting."

"It's a pleasure to meet you, Sam." Snegurka smiled and I was left standing in a marshmallow world, certain I would melt I felt so warm. "I'm Snegurka and this is my grandfather Ded Moroz, or Grandfather Frost."

It seemed all the Santas already knew Kertas, and after solemn offerings of sadness for the loss of his boss, Ded Moroz told us they remained in the North Pole because in Russia, Christmas was celebrated on the 7th of January.

"Like in Egypt," I said, recalling Baba Noël telling us the same thing.

"So Grandfather and I are in no rush to get home." Snegurka came closer to me, her blue eyes as piercing as the tip of a poinsettia. "We plan to stick around a few more days, enjoy a bit of relaxation before the final push. Perhaps build a snowman or two." She smiled at me in such a way I heard bells ringing and children singing.

"All is merry and bright tonight," I said waving my pipe at the sky above us. "Perhaps we could take a walk through the woods, see the holly and ivy when they are both full grown."

"I've always felt that of all the trees that are in the wood, the holly bears the crown."

"Holly and ivy," Kertas scoffed beside me, shaking his head. "Need me to pick up some mistletoe while you're out?"

I nudged Kertas with a pointed, branchy elbow.

"Or we could take a ride in a one-horse open sleigh, sing a song or two. I know a moose with access to one."

Snegurka giggled. "I'd like that."

Sheng Dan Lao Ren leaned closer to Kertas and mumbled, "I thought Nick preferred reindeer?"

"I'll explain later," Kertas responded with a grin in my direction.

"But I'm afraid our holly jolly Christmas will have to wait," Snegurka said, straightening and taking a step back. "Nick and Nora were looking for you two. They said you would find them at their house."

"Is it urgent?" I asked.

Ded Moroz and his granddaughter exchanged a glance and I knew I shouldn't have asked. It was tactless to think of things like sleigh rides when there was a murder to be solved.

"Come and find me when you're finished," Snegurka whispered, giving my branch arm a squeeze.

A thrill of hope went down my back as the stars shone even more brightly.

25

Return to the House of Claus

"Someone's hijacked the S-ANTA system."

Nick had waited only as long as it took for us to close the door behind us, clearly agitated by this news.

"What?!" Kertas yelled. "How? Why? Who?"

"Have a cup of cheer and take a seat," said Nora, handing Kertas a mug of hot cider that smelled almost as good as her cookies.

"Let's start at the beginning," I said.

"A very good place to start," said Nick, taking a seat across from us, as chilled as an Australian Christmas cheesecake. "It occurred to me that both Tannenbaums' murders must have something to do with the S-ANTA."

"It occurred to us, too," I said. "We've been asking every Santa we come across whether they use the system and what their thoughts are on it."

"Have you come up against anyone antagonistic toward it?"

Kertas and I exchanged a glance.

"I'd take that as a yes," said Nora.

"We've talked to so many people, let me pull out my notes." I removed my fedora and grabbed my notebook, no longer worried about keeping it secret from the others.

I was sure by now Kertas had caught me jotting down a thing or two, anyway, since while we'd traveled from place to place I'd made sure to take notes regarding our investigations thus far. Unfortunately, I hadn't had a chance to update it since speaking with Sheng Dan Lao Ren, Ded Moroz, and Snegurka, but I had a feeling nothing of great importance had been discussed with them. Nothing pertaining to the case at any rate.

"Let's see, we started with Père Noël and Baba Noël. They were cooking and Père Noël seemed pleased with the S-ANTA, though he didn't want to talk about Le Père Fouettard, and he dropped the flour when we said we were hunting down Tannenbaum's murderer."

"That seems rather crucial," said Nick. "Do you think he did it?"

I moved my pipe from one side to the other. "To be honest, I can't imagine any of the Santas behind the murders."

"But Fouettard?" Kertas suggested.

"I don't remember him, so I couldn't say, but you seem to rank him high in our suspects."

"Let's just say he's the type I wouldn't put it past. Perhaps it was an accident, a prank gone too far, but if we're speaking of character, I'd put my money on Fouettard."

"Just because a man dresses all in black and carries a whip doesn't mean he's going to poison someone," said Nick. "For heaven's sake, I used to carry a whip until I realized the reindeer didn't need any encouragement."

"A whip isn't always used for evil," said Nora in agreement with her husband. "I once knew a man who made a living singing along with a whip's cracks."

"Put a star next to Fouettard's name is all I'm saying," said Kertas, taking a sip of hot cider.

"Has anyone seen him?" I asked. "I mean, is he here in the North Pole?"

Everyone looked at one another as if to say, "Your guess is as good as mine."

"It doesn't take long to slip a bit of something into someone's drink," said Kertas quietly.

"You Yule Lads would know a thing or two about that," I said.

"What are you suggesting?" Kertas stood up quickly, his cider sloshing.

I raised my hands, still holding my pencil and notebook. "I'm not saying it was one of your brothers. What would they have to gain?"

"Except putting me, their brother, in a role of power in the North Pole?" Kertas glared.

I hadn't thought of that. "You said it, not me. But I don't think you did it, Kertas. We've already discussed this. Stop trying to make out I think you're guilty when I don't."

Kertas crossed his arms and harrumphed, realizing too late that this meant his cider went down his side and onto his lap.

"Let me get you a towel," said Nora, keeping awfully quiet about our whole exchange.

I wondered what the Clauses thought. Did they suspect Kertas this whole time? Was I the only one who didn't believe he'd murdered his boss, his boss's father, and his boss's lover?

Was I naive not to believe it?

When Nora returned with the towel, she suggested we join them for a meal. "I have a feeling this discussion is going to take most of the afternoon and into the evening. We haven't eaten yet and I assume, what with your investigating today, neither have you two."

"I can always eat," said Kertas, setting the damp towel at his side.

We adjourned to the dining room, the three of them each having a sandwich while I had an entire platter of Nora's magical cookies at my disposal. Then Nick tried to get us back on track.

"Who was next?" he asked. "You said Père Noël was with Baba Noël, who has only recently begun using the S-ANTA."

"He didn't seem antagonistic. It's not his fault only a few people in Egypt have Christmas trees. Just like Father Christmas, who didn't seem to have any issues with the S-ANTA. Sinterklaas, on the other hand, said he doesn't use the S-ANTA because the Piets have unionized and would never allow it."

Nick nodded. "Yeah, I've tried again and again to get them to see reason. If the Piets let Sinterklaas use the S-ANTA, it would mean less work for them."

"But they see less work as less reason for their existence," said Kertas. "It's the same problem with all technology. It's beneficial until it's not. The point of technology is to make life 'easier,' right? Yet inevitably it only makes it easier for some people, while taking away the livelihood of others. It's a delicate balance."

"One even Santa Claus has to consider," said Nick with a sad nod of his head.

"Babbo Natale and Papai Noel literally jumped when I suggested the Tannenbaums had been considering setting up a similar system through nativities, since that would reach a lot of the parts of the world where Christmas trees aren't as prevalent," I said.

Nick chuckled. "I would imagine so! Babbo and Papai aren't the only ones who'd react if he tried such a thing." He turned to Kertas. "Otmar wasn't thinking of doing that, was he? Because that would certainly make a lot of Santas upset..."

Kertas shook his head. "Not at all. It was just a ruse Shovel thought he'd suggest to see what sort of reaction he'd get. And he certainly got one: they both made noises like they didn't think the Tannenbaums' deaths had been such a great loss."

Nick sighed heavily. "It can't be..."

"What about Miss Plum?" Nora asked.

"We've focused on Ernst and Otmar," I said, "assuming the fairy died because she knew, or the murderer thought she knew, who had killed them."

"Based on the note we found in her pocket, I'd guess you're right about that," said Nick, taking a bite out of his sandwich.

"After we discovered Miss Plum this morning, we got off the S-ANTA track and followed some clues to Mrs. Cane.

Apparently, she had a secret side business with Tannenbaum to keep herself on top."

"Oh?" Nick and Nora said in unison.

"Mrs. Cane and Otmar Tannenbaum had come to an agreement in order to ensure his relationship with Miss Plum didn't affect the business side of things," I explained briefly.

"You mean candy canes vs. tinsel?" asked Nick.

"Yes."

"As a wise man once said, 'There's a lot of bad "isms" floatin' around this world, but one of the worst is commercialism,'" quoted Nora. "I'm not surprised. Mrs. Cane has always struck me as a shrewd businesswoman. Although, in my mind, it seems to me there's plenty of Christmas to go around for everyone."

"Here, here," said Nick, raising his glass of milk to his wife.

"Don't forget Rudolph's gambling arrangement with Mr. T," said Kertas.

"Right, we also spoke with the Gingerbread Man and the Nutcracker, too, but other than learning about all the things falling apart at the Nutcracker Suites, those were both dead ends," I said, coming to the end of my notes. "Just now we were speaking with Sheng Dan Lao Ren, who I know uses the S-ANTA, but didn't seem to have any problems with it—"

"That reminds me!" Kertas reached under his hat and pulled out his Peace Apple, taking a mighty crunch out of it and waving his hand indicating I continue.

"—and the same goes for Ded Moroz and Snegurka, who are clearly not murderers."

"Oh?" the Clauses said together again, giving me a look I didn't appreciate.

"There's no way Snegurka has had anything to do with any of this. Why would she?" If a snowman could blush, I knew I would have been. That warm feeling was filling my chest again, and it wasn't just Nora's hot cocoa cookies.

"So you think the whole S-ANTA connection is just a red herring?" Nick asked.

"I was starting to think so," I said. "Until you brought us here and said the S-ANTA's been hijacked."

26

Hijacked

"All I know is someone has commandeered the system. It's delivering something other than gifts, but I can't tell what," said Nick.

"How do you know?"

"The machine is located in a warehouse attached to the back of the Tannenbaum factory, so I went over and thought I'd take a look at it. I was really worried it would somehow know its inventor had died and would refuse to work out of grief."

"The S-ANTA is sentient?" I lifted my twig eyebrows, not too surprised if the answer was yes, given my own existence.

"No, no, nothing like that." Nick hesitated. "At least, not that I know of." He looked to Kertas.

The gnome shook his head. "It's not gonna go all HAL on you and say, 'I'm sorry, Santa, I can't do that.'"

"You never know around here," said Nick with a shrug. "I thought it worth checking anyway, and since I wasn't sure where you two had ended up, I decided to check on it myself."

"And you found something."

"Yes. I was able to log in like normal, and everything looked just fine to start. Then this message popped up asking me if I'd like to accept all cookies. You know how every website has a disclaimer these days. So I pushed yes."

Kertas paused mid-bite on his apple. "It said what?"

Nick sighed and blew out his rosy cheeks. "I know now it was false."

"It was a bug? A virus?" I asked, though even as I said it I wasn't certain how I even knew what that was.

"Apparently, yeah, something like that, because all of a sudden the screen went blank and I worried I'd broken it. Then everything came back up and looked just fine. I went ahead and ran a diagnostic just to be sure and that was when it told me there had been an update."

"What update?" Kertas asked.

"Twenty-five something. I don't remember the exact number. I decided to call up the log." He turned to me. "We each have a personal code for logging in to the system, so I could see when each of us had logged in and what changes had been made."

"'We' who?" I asked. "You, Kertas, the Tannenbaums, who else had a code?"

"Franklin," said Kertas, his apple forgotten in his hand. "If that turkey—"

"It wasn't Franklin. At least, his code was nowhere to be seen, not since Ernst's death. But someone else's code was," said Nick.

"Stop pausing for dramatic emphasis and tell us who," said Nora, voicing my thoughts exactly and making me smile in spite of the tension.

Nick looked directly at Kertas. "Ernst."

"Ernst," Kertas repeated.

"Ernst?" Nora asked.

"You mean he's not dead?" I asked, avoiding saying the man's name a fourth time.

Nick kept looking at Kertas. "You tell me."

Kertas waved his hand so dramatically the apple core went flying back over his shoulder, landing in what to me was a rather comfy-looking snowdrift, but might have been a couch to the rest of them.

"Ernst Tannenbaum has been dead for two years. I promise you. Unless that moose lied to me, both of my bosses are dead as doornails, though what's so dead about a doornail I'll never know, dead as a coffin-nail is more like it," he finished with a grumbling mutter.

Nick nodded once. "All right then, there's only one other option."

"He's a ghost," I breathed.

"No, no." Nick laughed. "Someone must have stolen his login, or guessed it. That's why I said someone hijacked the system. From what I could tell, according to the dates, they've been logging in every month or so since Ernst's death and changing something in the code. The problem is: I can't tell what." Again, Nick turned to Kertas. "I was hoping you could help me figure that part out."

Kertas shrugged. "I don't know anything."

"You've inherited the business and the system, I assumed Otmar had taught you how to run the S-ANTA."

"A little," said the gnome. "But just because I know how to use a computer doesn't mean I understand the code that makes it do what it's doing. I'm no IT whiz. I know how to log in and push buttons just like you, Nick, but I have no idea how Mr. T made the S-ANTA do what it does. I guess he never thought he'd die before passing on the handbook." He snapped his fingers. "Maybe there's a handbook somewhere."

Nick shook his head. "Not that I could find. I just spent the last hour or so looking for one. That was the next thing I did after realizing what had happened."

"So there's no way to see who was logging in?" I asked.

"Nope. As far as the computer's concerned, it was Ernst, but since we know that can't be true..." Nick opened his hands and sighed.

"Can we check for fingerprints?"

"Not everyone around here has them, and I don't want to go around printing everyone as though I suspect them."

"But you do suspect them. Everyone in the North Pole is a suspect."

"We're only two days from Christmas. The last thing I want to do is ruin the Christmas spirit by sowing doubt and suspicion everywhere."

"It's happening already whether you like it or not," Kertas grumbled.

"We're not checking for fingerprints," said Nick firmly. "That's final."

I'd never seen Santa look so serious. And I never wanted to again.

He turned to his wife. "I'm sorry, Nora, did you have a good lunch?"

"It's the nicest lunch I ever listened to," said Nora with a smile.

Nick sighed heavily and stood up from the table. "I suppose the next thing I can do is call the remaining Santas together for an emergency meeting. Perhaps one of them has noticed something strange being delivered alongside the presents coming through the S-ANTA."

A few hours later, we'd gathered around the fire once again, though Kertas and I stood outside the inner glow, for my safety and to keep an eye on the gathered Santas. I hoped one of them would admit what he'd done quickly. Two days was two days too long to be suspecting everyone I met of something so heinous. I wished I'd never laid eyes on that Sugar Plum fairy. Of all the snowbanks in all the towns in all the world, why'd she have to walk into mine?

"It's come down to this," said Nick, summing up his speech. "Clearly, whoever killed Ernst Tannenbaum and Otmar Tannenbaum hijacked the S-ANTA for his own personal use, and when Miss Sugar Plum discovered his name, she was silenced before she could tell me. The hijacker and murderer could be sitting here amongst us even now, in this very circle. Can you pass the fish?"

This last remark was directed at Babbo Natale, who'd brought some of the *lutefisk* that Sinterklaas had gifted him to share with everyone, most likely because the Italian Santa didn't care for the fish himself.

Many of the Santas had left already, so around the fire in addition to the Clauses there only remained Baba Noël, Sheng Dan Lao Ren, Babbo Natale, Ded Moroz, and Snegurka.

"Could this be the cause of the unbelief?" Ded Moroz asked.

"What do you mean?" Nick asked.

"It seems to me that fewer and fewer children are believing in Santa Claus these days," the Russian Santa said with a sad shake of his head. "I worry what will become of us."

Nick swallowed his bite of *lutefisk*. "What I've found is if you do good deeds, you inspire others to do the same. It's the gift that keeps on giving. In the end, I don't have to continue delivering Everywhere because others take it upon themselves to continue the magic. That's why the franchise system works and the S-ANTA."

"And the parents? The ones spreading the lie that you—we—don't exist?" Baba Noël asked. "That doesn't concern you?"

"To be honest, it does. I do worry. But not that we'll cease to be needed. The name Santa Claus is so connected with the Christmas Spirit at this point, if people stopped believing in me, I'm more worried about what *else* they would stop believing in." Nick sighed and took a seat on a log.

The other Santas murmured amongst themselves.

"In the end, however," Nick said softly, "it's not my job to make people believe. You can lead a reindeer to water but you can't make him drink."

The ring of Santas was quiet except for the soft rustling of robes as they shifted their feet.

"Do you think it more likely that one of the Santas who was

here but has left is the culprit?" Sheng Dan Lao Ren asked, his hands tucked into the long sleeves of his hanfu. "Perhaps one of them killed that poor fairy, then ran home before he could be brought to justice?"

Nick glanced in the direction of me and Kertas and I shrugged. Sheng made a good point. It was much more likely that the murderer had done his evil deed, then fled the scene. In fact, he could have done so in regards to all three murders, since this meeting of the Santas was an annual event.

"Who is missing?" I whispered to Kertas.

Kertas's eyes roved over the collected Santas like a child counting his presents under the tree. "Well, quite a few, but the one whose absence interests me the most is der Weihnachtsmann."

"Der Weihnachtsmann," I repeated, the name sounding dark and mysterious itself. "Isn't he the one at the meeting yesterday with the caped hood who reminded me of the Ghost of Christmas Future?"

"I could see that, yeah."

"We never talked to him."

"Exactly. He left before he could be questioned. Because he's guilty?"

27

Believe

"Der Weihnachtsmann is back home in Germany by now," said Nick with a shake of his head. "We can try to contact him, but tomorrow is the day before Christmas Eve. We're cutting it awful close with this whole thing."

The other Santas had been given leave to disperse, returning to the Nutcracker Suites as the night closed in, a darkness that seemed to encroach on the fire around which we'd been standing.

"Which is why I didn't want you bothering with it in the first place, Nicky," said Nora. She sighed and rubbed above her eyes. "But now I see I couldn't have stopped you from becoming involved any more than Max could stop the Grinch. You have to play the role you're given."

"Thank you for understanding, sweetheart," said Nick, giving his wife a kiss on the forehead.

She smiled up at him and tapped his nose. "Just don't forget your first role is Santa Claus. As the head Santa, you've got to prepare for Christmas Eve as much as the rest of them."

"Will do." Nick saluted. "On that note, I suggest we all get a good night's rest and greet this thing with fresh eyes in the morning. Would you care to pull up a snowball here, Sam? You're welcome to it."

"I think I just might. Thanks, Nick," I said.

"I suppose you won't be needing this." Nick began to pack a large snowball to douse the fire, but Kertas stopped him.

"I think I'll stick it out with Shovel tonight—if that's all right with you?" he asked me.

"Fine with me," I said with a smile. I was glad I wouldn't be left alone with my thoughts again tonight.

"Shall we play it again, Sam?" he asked as Nick and Nora disappeared arm-in-arm into the darkness.

"You mean should we begin making 'the mountains in reply echoing our brief delight...'"

"'Us—they are green when summer days are bright...'"

"'-er visions beam afar...'"

"Good one," said Kertas.

"Thanks." It was tricky coming up with a line from another Christmas carol that picked up where the last line left off, but thanks to my memory returning a little more each day, I knew I could keep my gnome friend on his toes.

"Let's see, 'afar...' How about: 'field and fountain, moor and mountain, following yonder star...'"

"'With royal beauty bright, westward—"

"You can't use the same song."

"Who says?"

"I do. It's too easy. It's practically the same line even."

"Fine," I admitted. "Then I'll say: 'in the sky looked down where He lay...'"

"Works for me. 'Keeping their sheep...'"

We continued on like this well into the night, until Kertas succumbed to his gnomely need for sleep, and the light of the fire finally dwindled as I watched.

I wasn't certain it was morning when my thoughts were interrupted by the crunching of footprints in the snow from the other side of the fire.

I tapped Kertas on the shoulder.

"Do you hear what I hear?" I asked, tipping my chin toward the sound and squinting my eyes, hoping to see through the darkness.

"'The angel voices...'" Kertas turned over on his snowbank and pulled his hat lower over his eyes.

"No, no." I shook him harder. "I'm not playing anymore. You fell asleep."

"I did not," he grumbled, sitting up and scratching his bald head before replacing his hat.

"Did, too. You've been asleep for hours. I heard something just now."

"It's just the fire settling."

"It's not that. It's—"

The crunching sound grew louder.

Kertas stood up and peered in the direction I had been looking.

"We hear you!" he yelled toward the trees. "No need to sneak. Come out and introduce yourself."

"I ain't afraid of no Christmas ghosts," I yelled, too, just to be sure whoever it was knew he wouldn't be making me jump anytime soon.

"I am no ghost," said a deep voice from directly behind us.

Those ten lords a-leaping had nothing on this one gnome a-vaulting.

"Son of a nutcracker! Mundang noodle! You—"

"I apologize. I did not mean to frighten you."

I tried to hide my smile as Kertas continued in his tirade.

"Der Weihnachtsmann, I presume," I said with a small bow, which was reciprocated by the tall, broad man in a scarlet cowl.

He lowered his peaked hood to reveal a pale face encircled by the puffiest, softest-looking white beard I'd seen yet, which he continued to produce from beneath the cowl's neckline, rippling from his chin into a cloud-like formation across his chest.

"I let the whiskers out as much as possible," der Weihnachtsmann said, his upturned lips pleased by my obvious appreciation. "Cold air makes them grow."

His eyes twinkled merrily as he watched Kertas still dealing with his bewilderment.

"Needless to say, we're surprised to see you here," I said. "Tomorrow's Christmas Eve."

"I know, but I had to come as soon as I heard. If you're quite finished, we have much business to attend to." The German Santa handed something to Kertas.

Something green and oblong. "A pickle?"

"*Frohe Weihnachten*," said the Santa. "In my country, people hide a pickle in the Christmas tree and the first child to find it gets an extra present. I hope it will bring you joy."

"It's a pickle," said Kertas.

Der Weihnachtsmann lifted a finger. "A pickle *candle*." He smiled.

Kertas grinned from ear to ear and took a large bite out of the green thing. "It really is!" he declared, bouncing on the tips of his toes out of pleasure now rather than surprise.

"Our Christmastime began on *Nikolaustag*—St. Nicholas Day—December 6th, so I have had many nights of making deliveries, tucking presents into children's shoes. I had almost completely finished my deliveries when I discovered something."

"What?" I asked, leaning forward in anticipation.

"The children have always left letters for me in their shoes, which I then replace with the gifts. When I explained this to Mr. Tannenbaum he agreed to arrange it so the S-ANTA not only delivered the gifts into the shoes, but also would retrieve the letters for me. It's been working quite wonderfully, which is why I feel confident in reporting to you even though today is my last day to make in-person deliveries."

"If you're worried the S-ANTA will stop working so well since Mr. T's death, you needn't have bothered. We've checked on that already," said Kertas, licking his fingers and eyeing der Weihnachtsmann's cloak like he hoped he had another couple candles hidden inside.

"No, no, I know it is working fine, more than fine." The German Santa waved his hand. "And by more than fine, I mean the S-ANTA appears to be delivering more than presents."

I glanced to Kertas. This was exactly what we'd been looking for. "What's it delivering?"

"Cookies."

I frowned. "Cookies? How do you know? Don't your children set out cookies for Santa? Or if not cookies, some sort of treat—whatever the German version of *kahk* or *pepernoten* is?"

Der Weihnachtsmann shook his head. "It's tradition to leave the letters, not the cookies. But lately, there's been gingerbread."

I recalled Merry telling us his original name had been a German one. "*Lebkuchen*," I said aloud.

Der Weihnachtsmann's eyebrows rose. "Correct. Now, I didn't think anything of it for the past couple years—"

"This has been happening for years?"

The German Santa shrugged. "Yes, but I simply assumed that, like most Western Christmas traditions, it was something brought over from the United States that the children of my country had decided to incorporate. There is nothing pernicious about gingerbread."

"Except Nick said whoever hijacked the S-ANTA has been doing it since the death of Ernst Tannenbaum two years ago," I murmured to Kertas.

"There's more to it than gingerbread, though," said der Weihnachtsmann. "It's what's been added to the gingerbread. I only made the connection tonight—or last night since it's now morning—and I've been traveling back here ever since."

"If time is relative to Santa Claus, why couldn't you have arrived at the moment you left?" I asked.

Der Weihnachtsmann frowned. "We are still restricted by time, even if it is relative to us. We are not time travelers.

We cannot travel backwards on our own timeline, otherwise we would have extended our work to before the original St. Nicholas."

"Oh," I said, nodding as though that made sense.

"But that does not matter. Listen to what I am telling you: someone has added something terrible to the gingerbread."

"Pickles?" Kertas asked.

"Worse. It's making parents believe that there is no Santa Claus!"

"I thought parents have always struggled with unbelief?" Even I remembered enough to know that. "The older a person gets, the more difficult it is for them to believe in magic. It's the basis of pretty much every Christmas movie concerning Santa Claus ever made."

"*Miracle on 34th Street* is my favorite," said Kertas. "Makes me cry every time."

"Yes, yes, it's always been around," said der Weihnachtsmann. "But this is *emphasizing* that unbelief, it's spreading the lie, blocking their sensors. I don't understand it completely, but then, I'm no baker."

"You're telling me there's a spice out there that has the ability of dulling someone's belief?" I asked incredulously.

Der Weihnachtsmann lifted his hands in the air. "I suppose there must be."

"We need to speak with someone intimately familiar with the properties of cookies." I turned to Kertas.

"One name springs to mind," said Kertas.

28

Let It Snow

"I'm afraid this is where I leave you," said the German Santa, lifting his peaked hood over his head and tucking his whiskers back beneath the neckline of his cowl.

"But someone has to tell the Clauses," I said.

"I must return to Germany. My children open their presents on Christmas Eve—tomorrow! *Frohe Weihnachten und viel Glück!*" he said, then crunched off into the woods the way he'd come.

We waved farewell and turned to each other.

"You go to the Clauses and I'll go to The Gingerbread House," said Kertas.

"No, no, the opposite."

"You'll melt at The Gingerbread House in a second," argued Kertas. "At the Clauses you can stay nice and cool and send them to meet me there."

"Fine," I agreed. I turned to go when something came sailing out of the woods and crashed directly through my lower-most snowball, sending me face down once more onto the ground.

"Not again," I muttered into the snow. "A little help?" I called out. "I can't get up." I paused. "I can't get up," I said again, only then realizing my voice was so muffled it sounded like "Rum pum pum pum."

I waited a few seconds. When Kertas didn't immediately reach down to help me up like last time, I felt in the pits of my coals that something was wrong.

"Kertas?" I tried to call.

No answer.

Carefully, I tried to push myself up on my branch arms. They were stronger than they looked, thankfully, and the snow was not the type to cling to me like before, so I was able to lift myself relatively easily once I gave it a go. I found the hole in my body and patched myself up as before.

"Kertas?" I called again.

I looked about and almost cried out when I saw Kertas lying face-down in the snow to my right, his crumpled Santa hat a few feet before him.

I slid alongside him and reached down to roll him over. "Kertas, Kertas, get up!"

A groan escaped the gnome. His face was blue with cold.

"What happened?" he moaned.

"Misfortune seems our lot. You fell into a drifted bank."

"Don't be upset. I'll be all right."

"Something went through me and hit you. Maybe another brick?" I looked around for the offending item. "Nope, just a rock this time." I held up a round gray stone the size of a Christmas tree star.

"My head," Kertas groaned, grabbing his forehead on either side as he tried to sit up.

"Where did it hit you?"

"I donno," Kertas mumbled, patting his beard down his front and feeling himself over for any broken bones.

"Can you stand?"

The gnome tried to get to his feet, but stumbled and went down with a plop. "Fa la la la. Looks like you'll have to go for help."

"If we can get you standing, I think you could lean on me to walk. I'm sturdier than I look." I patted my packed snow.

I took Kertas by the hand and he hoisted himself to his feet, this time placing all his weight only on his left foot, keeping his right foot aloft.

"Can you grab my hat?" he asked.

I tentatively reached for it while at the same time trying to give him support. We eventually succeeded, though Kertas ended up on his rump again for a minute.

Once we were gathered and situated, we began the long slide-hop-step to the Clauses'.

"Ho, there!" a voice shouted behind us, and I turned to find Dr. Flick treading boldly in our footsteps. "I see the t-t-two of you are heedless of the wind and weather headed this way. Or are you m-m-making your way to shelter as we speak?"

"It's only just begun snowing," I said, putting my branch out to catch a few falling flakes.

I looked up at the sky, though I now realized it was much darker than usual by day. I could not see the moon or the stars, which implied a great cloud had blotted them out.

"A storm's m-m-moving in. Hopefully it will p-p-pass before tomorrow night, but in the meantime, I recommend we all s-s-seek the indoors, even you, s-s-snowman."

"A little snow never hurt a snowman," I said jauntily, but even as I spoke, I could feel the change in the air.

The moose gave a great shake of his antlers, releasing the collected snow.

"Kertas has done something to his foot, and we need to get news to the Clauses right away," I said.

"Let me have a l-l-look." The moose examined Kertas's leg, much to the gnome's chagrin. Kertas grimaced and gasped as the moose tried to touch him. "I can't tell if it's a s-s-sprain or a f-f-fracture. I need more light." He straightened his glasses. "Perhaps I could r-r-run ahead with Kertas and t-t-tell N-n-nick your news?"

I almost took the moose into our confidences. All we knew so far was that someone had tampered with the gingerbread cookies, but as I'd seen at the tinsel factory, Christmas tree emporium, and candy cane farm, security was anything but tight around here. Anyone could have snuck in and tampered with the cookies and then somehow reprogrammed the S-ANTA. Since I was still unsure who was precisely behind all this, I thought it best to keep what we'd learned from der Weihnachtsmann to ourselves.

It seemed Kertas felt the same, or he was in too much pain to argue, leaving it up to me as I deliberated, the snow falling thicker by the minute.

"Kertas can tell Nick," I said. "But if you'd be so kind as to carry him there, I think you'll both travel a lot quicker on your four legs. I've got to go another direction, anyway."

Kertas nodded as I spoke, so I took it that he agreed with my decision. I leaned down and helped him up onto the moose's back.

"Good luck, Kertas. Send Nick to The Gingerbread House as soon as the storm lifts. I'll meet him there."

"You got it. Careful, Shovel. Every cookie's got its crumbling point."

I gave a short nod. Dr. Flick told Kertas to hang on tight to his sweater collar and they were off.

The snow swirled before the hanging lamps, lanterns, and strings of Christmas lights along the path as I turned around and headed back the way we'd come.

I was glad I was a snowman in this weather. Dr. Flick hadn't been kidding. While we'd been distracted by our conversation with der Weihnachtsmann, a storm had been building around us. The streets were empty as I made my way, pressing through the fresh drifts of snow until I finally spied the lighted windows of The Gingerbread House in the distance. Carefully skirting the Milky Lake to my left, I finally came to the front door of the house.

I knocked.

No one answered.

I knocked again, more forcefully. "Hello? Hello!" I called. "Is someone there?"

The door cracked open and a small face peeked out, bringing the smell of cloves, nutmeg, cinnamon, cardamom, and all those glorious spices that would have brought me to my knees —if I'd had knees.

"Mr. Snowman!" the face squeaked as the door opened wider. It was the little squirrel whom I'd met outside the Tannenbaum factory, dressed now in yellow worker's coveralls dusted with flour. "Come in, come in!" she cried, waving me through.

I stepped inside and immediately felt warmer, which gave me visions of melting sugar plums, rather than dancing ones.

"What are you doing out on a day like today?" the squirrel asked.

"I need to speak with Merry. Is he in?" I asked.

"Oh, no, I'm afraid he left to deliver some cookies to the Nutcracker Suites. They're always running short, especially with so many Santas staying over thanks to the storm. I do hope they can get home in time for Christmas. My husband says I shouldn't worry about things that haven't happened yet, but I say—"

"I'm sorry, but I can't stay long." I knew it was rude to cut her off, but I also knew if I stayed in this hot factory too long I'd become a puddle and wouldn't be any help to anyone. "I'll just go find him at the hotel. Thank you..." I leaned in to try to read the name on her name tag. "Fragile."

"It's pronounced 'fra-gee-lay.' It's Italian." The squirrel smiled.

"As I said, thank you for your help, but I really must be going." I made to open the door just a crack and the storm whirled through, blowing out candles nearby and causing other workers to scramble and squeak.

The squirrel slammed the door and threw the bolt.

"You're not going anywhere," Fragile squeaked.

For a minute, my heart sank. Could *she* be the one who'd poisoned the cookies?

"I'll not let you blow away outside in this storm. Come along with me." She grabbed my hand and began pulling me back into the depths of the factory.

We passed aisles of ingredients and aisles of workbenches, on which I saw little gingerbread men being decorated, their eyes, smiles, and buttons being applied quickly and efficiently by the small hands of squirrels, chipmunks, red pandas, ferrets, chinchillas, pygmy marmosets, and others.

"Where are we going?" I asked.

"You'll see..."

My heart thumped as loudly as the machines I heard mixing and plopping out batter to bake. I was thankful when I realized we seemed to be heading in the opposite direction of the enormous ovens I saw lining the far walls, but I still worried about the squirrel's disinclination to tell me her plan.

"I really think—"

"I think you'll be quite safe in here," Fragile said with a proud grin as she presented our destination.

The freezer.

I let out the huge breath I hadn't realized I'd been holding.

"Perfect," I said with a relieved smile. "Thank you."

"No problem! I'll come and get you when the storm passes."

"Thank you, seriously," I said, and let myself into the walk-in freezer.

It wasn't large. Obviously the factory didn't use a lot of frozen items, though I figured the fridge was probably packed to the brim with eggs, milk, and the like.

The door swung shut behind me and after a moment, I heard a small click.

I turned and realized the window looking out on the factory was frozen over, so I couldn't see. I reached for the handle, intending to lean out to remind Fragile that she should come get me whenever Merry returned.

The handle wouldn't budge. I was locked in the freezer.

"Oh, fudge."

29

Frozen

At least I couldn't die here. Eventually someone would come along to grab an ingredient and they'd let me out.

All I had to do was wait.

And so I did.

For hours.

Apparently, not many ingredients need to be frozen when it comes to cookies.

I had time to catalog what was in the freezer, and I'll admit, there wasn't much outside of ice, ice cream, and fruit. Perhaps they made ice cream cookies during the summer, but in the winter, there was hardly any call for cold items. Everyone wanted hot.

Sure, in the countries on the other side of the world it was currently summer, so there would be popsicles and ice cream and meringues and cheesecake. But here at the North Pole, where it would be dark and freezing for six months, then suddenly light and freezing for six months, there was little to no call for frozen food.

Every once in awhile I called out, "Hello?" but I knew it was a feeble attempt. No doubt the thick walls made it practically impossible for sound to carry out into the factory.

Fragile had said she'd let me out when the storm blew over. There was nothing I could do until then.

I settled in next to a pile of boxes labeled "cranberries."

The first thought that went through my mind was the hope that Kertas and Dr. Flick had arrived at the Clauses' house safely. Most likely, they, too, were making a plan just as I was, and thinking through everything we knew so far.

I pulled out my notebook and added what der Weihnachtsmann had told us. Then I began a new page with the heading *What We Know.*

1. The S-ANTA has been reprogrammed to deliver cookies as well as gifts.
2. The S-ANTA only works if the country uses Christmas trees.

But there was no classification for countries that also set out cookies or treats of some sort for Santa to eat. The program assumed both went hand-in-hand, which was how der Weihnachtsmann was able to realize something had changed.

I recalled what our conversations about *kahk* had led to with all the Santas. I added to my list:

3. Almost all countries have a spiced cookie of some sort.

This was important because it meant even if the country didn't make gingerbread itself, per say, it was the sort of cookie that could be snuck in without drawing a lot of attention.

4. The cookies have had something added to them to make parents stop believing in Santa Claus.

That, right there, was the Big Issue at hand. This was bigger than murder, even.

Okay, maybe not that big, but up here it sure felt like it. If the folks down south stopped believing in Santa Claus, our entire reason for living went up in smoke.

And if this Someone could figure out how to reprogram the S-ANTA to sneak in cookies that caused *parents* to stop believing...how long would it be before the *children* stopped believing, too?

I sighed heavily. I wondered if the reason the cookies had only worked so far on parents was because it was standard practice for the parents to eat the cookies left out by the kids for Santa Claus in order to encourage the "myth."

The real Santas never ate everything left for them. They'd all be enormous if that were true. Unless weight was relative like time to them. I'd always wondered about that. I began to make a note to ask Nick the next time I saw him, but then I erased it.

I had bigger questions to answer right now. The biggest being Who Was Behind This?

I considered the facts, and ended right back where Kertas and I had been as soon as der Weihnachtsmann had said it had to do with cookies.

It had to be someone at The Gingerbread House.

Could it be Fragile herself? Last time I'd seen her, she'd been standing outside the Tannenbaum offices, mindlessly twiddling her thumbs, or so I'd thought. She'd claimed to be waiting for her husband, but what if she'd really just left the body of Otmar Tannenbaum in the forest, after making certain her poison had done its work the night before?

Squirrels were known for their quiet scurrying. She could have snuck in and dropped a bit of mistletoe into his eggnog without anyone noticing. Same for Ernst and his tea.

But why? Was it as simple as a domino effect? Had she tampered with the S-ANTA, which had been discovered by Ernst, so he had to die, and then Otmar had discovered she'd killed his father, so he'd had to die, and then Miss Plum had discovered she'd killed both Tannenbaums, so *she'd* had to die...

And now I'd figured it out, so I had to die.

I jiggled the handle on the freezer door one more time.

Nothing.

The thing was, if Fragile had wanted to kill me, it wouldn't have been exceedingly difficult. It didn't take a lot of ingenuity to kill a snowman. You only needed one ingredient. Heat. All she had to do was to lead me through the factory by way of the ovens. I could see it now:

"Oh, I'm so sorry! I wasn't thinking! I was taking him to the freezer, I swear! It was an accident!" Her fake tears streaming down her furry face as she spoke, her nimble fingers reaching for a handkerchief to hide her smug little smile. "I don't know what happened!"

I shook my head. She could have done that. But she hadn't.

Instead, she'd led me straight to the freezer, giving the ovens a wide berth.

I was almost certain Fragile wasn't the murderer.

Besides, why would she reprogram the S-ANTA?

Had she been let down as a child? Had she bottled up a secret hatred of Santa Claus, causing her to vow to end the entire enterprise and destroy Santa once and for all?

If so, she was a marvelous actor. Then again, you could hide a lot behind a smile.

I thought of Nuss Knacker at the Nutcracker Suites and his painted grin. He couldn't let his true nature show even if he wanted to. Such was the way of nutcrackers.

And cookies. Specifically, gingerbread men.

I pictured Merry, with his licorice smile stuck on with frosting. Was he even capable of letting it curve down instead of up?

What might he be hiding behind that smile? Behind the happy-go-lucky attitude of "cookies make everyone happy"?

He'd certainly had access. We'd run into Merry everywhere we'd gone, since he liked to make his cookie deliveries himself. He delivered to the Tannenbaums, and both of them had enjoyed cookies with their drinks. What if the poison hadn't been in the drinks at all?

Dr. Flick had said the poison was in Otmar Tannenbaum's system, but he hadn't been able to find the source since Kertas had cleaned the mug. In his stomach had been the ingredients of a cookie: "flour, sugar, butter...and a wide variety of spices from cinnamon to c-c-cardamom," the doc had said.

Merry had been at the tinsel factory, too. When we'd arrived, Silver Leaf had said Merry had just delivered a fresh batch of cookies for the fairies overnight. What was to say he hadn't snuck back after dropping them off, to have a little chat with a certain fairy he thought might know his secret?

There'd even been crumbs around her body. At the time, I'd assumed they were from the cookie she'd been eating, but now I wondered if Merry hadn't placed that cookie in her hand to hide the evidence in plain sight, knowing there was no way to hide the crumbs that would naturally fall from him as he killed her, which would lead us to suspect him.

And when it came to the S-ANTA cookies, the ones with a super secret ingredient, well... If anyone knew a thing or two about cookies, it was Merry.

30

Merry Christmas

The storm must have raged an entire day and a half, or so it seemed to me locked in my little frozen cell.

I kept reminding myself it could have been worse.

I kept reminding myself that someone had to come eventually.

I kept reminding myself that the Someone who came might be Merry himself.

What would I say to him when I saw him?

"Merry Christmas, you filthy animal."

Thankfully, it wasn't Merry who finally opened the door.

"Shovel! You're all right! We've been looking all over for

you!" Kertas hobbled across the icy floor of the freezer toward me.

"Careful!" I said. "Don't slip and sprain your other leg."

"I'm okay. Dr. Flick wrapped it up good. We've been out searching for you ever since the storm cleared. It never occurred to me that you might be *inside* The Gingerbread House." He glanced around. "I see you found the one place safe enough for a snowman in a bakery."

"Not by any fault of my own," I said. "I was locked in."

"Locked in?" Kertas went back to the door, which had naturally shut behind him. Thankfully it opened as soon as he pushed on the handle. "It wasn't locked just now."

"Strawberry cheesecake, are you serious?" I leapt across the freezer. "He must have released the lock when he saw you coming. Didn't want to get caught with his hand in the cookie jar."

"Who?"

"Merry Christmas."

"Technically, it's Christmas Eve," Kertas said.

"No, no, Merry, the Gingerbread Man. He's the one behind this whole thing."

"Are you sure?"

"Yes, I've figured it all out. Trust me, I've had plenty of time to do so." I explained my thought process as I led the way out of the freezer, assuming Kertas would follow in my wake. When I made to turn down the third aisle, I glanced behind me to find he was indeed trying to keep up as well as he could.

"Go on, go on," he said with a wave of his hands. "I'll catch up."

I nodded and made for the door. No way I was going to stay

in this place another minute. I'd had enough of gingerbread for a lifetime.

Once outside, I paused and considered my options. Since he'd locked me in the freezer, I assumed Merry knew I knew what he'd done. But he'd also *un*locked me, so either he knew there was no point in running, or he had something else up his frosting sleeve.

Kertas joined me as I turned in a circle. "'You know, maybe he's only a little crazy like painters or composers or...or some of those men in Washington.'"

"*Miracle on 34th Street*?"

"I told you it was my favorite." Kertas shrugged.

"Tannenbaum's Christmas Tree Emporium, the candy cane farm, the tinsel factory, the Nutcracker Suites, the forest... Where are you, you little cookie?" I muttered.

"Right here," said a voice to my right.

I turned.

Merry sat, a basket of cookies beside him, on a little bench alongside Milky Lake.

The feeling of something inevitable swept over me.

"Why are you still here?"

"Did you expect me to run?"

"Well, you are the Gingerbread Man."

"Run, run, as fast as you can, you can't catch me, I'm the Gingerbread Man."

I slid closer. "Something like that."

"I wasn't always this way." His eyes got a dark, inner look as he gazed out over the lake. "Oma Perchta was run over on this exact day fifty-three years ago by Nick Claus himself," he said slowly. "I almost died, but in the end, I only lost a leg. Nick felt so terrible about what happened, he charged the bakers here at the North Pole with putting their heads together and figuring out a way to bake me a new one. He even offered to set me up with a full-time job, that of running The Gingerbread House. They thought I was grateful. I let them think that. It was easier than trying to explain that I could never forgive Santa Claus for what he'd done. I vowed that when I grew up, I'd ensure there were no more Santa Clauses. Anywhere."

"But...you've been living here all this time?"

"Yes, yes, ironic isn't it? Is that the correct use of the word? I can never remember. But yes, I had to join the very industry I had vowed to dismantle. I tried a few different ways, and every time, I lost another part of myself."

Physically and mentally, I thought.

"This time, though." He rubbed his hands together. "This time has worked like a charm, and with absolutely no harm to myself. Now that Nick Claus has accepted all cookies, there's no way to un-do the program I created in the S-ANTA. My work here is done. Families everywhere will forget there really is a Santa Claus—parents and children alike. The entire industry will crumble beneath their fingers." He held up his cookie hands. "Much like my own."

"I don't understand. How could you live here so long and not learn anything about the true meaning of Christmas?"

The Gingerbread Man laughed. "What is this? A Hallmark film? The only thing I've learned while living at the North Pole is that humanity is the same everywhere in the world. From end to end it is covered by people craving selfish power. From Tannenbaum's little side deal with the Canes to Rudolph's gambling addiction to Nick Claus setting himself up as the head Santa Claus over all the others, there is nothing new under the sun, or under the moon for that matter." He waved toward the sky as he spoke, his candy eyes sparkling with madness in the starlight.

"Frau Perchta must've loved having you for a grandson," muttered Kertas. "You're insane."

"Am I? Perhaps I am. Aren't all inventors just a little insane? You have to be to think outside the chocolate box. What better mind to come up with something like the S-ANTA?"

I blinked. "You invented the S-ANTA? I thought—"

"Yes, yes, you thought the Tannenbaums invented it. That's just another proof in the Christmas pudding. You see, really I was the one who had the idea. Genius, isn't it? But what's even more genius is letting the Tannenbaums think *they* invented it. No fingers pointing back to me."

"You let them? Wouldn't you prefer people knew the real brains behind it all?"

Merry shook his head. "Nope, not when the real invention was sneaking my code into the machine. You see, before I became more cookie than man, I was just a young boy with a mind for computers, so when the S-ANTA began to be built, it was a simple matter to enter my code so that gingerbread cookies, as well as presents, were being delivered. Only to some stations, you understand, not all. And there was nothing in the cookies just yet. That was to be added later. It was slow and steady work, but then, all the best bakers know it takes time to perfect a recipe."

"So you've been sneaking cookies in for decades."

"Yes."

"But then, why did you kill Mr. T's father?" Kertas asked.

"He must have figured it out," I said.

"Precisely." Merry pointed to his frosting nose. "Bravo, Shovel, bravo." The cookie stood and looked out across the lake once more. "Ernst returned from one of his annual trips to check on the S-ANTA and somewhere along the way, he must have realized my cookies were being added. Thankfully, he gave me a chance to turn off the code. 'Because it's Christmas,' he said." The Gingerbread Man shook his head like this was the silliest thing he'd ever heard of. "He should have banished me when he had the chance."

"Then Otmar Tannenbaum figured it out?"

"Apparently I wasn't as sneaky as I thought." Merry turned and frowned. "This year I hit a hiccup or three. Otmar returned from his trip this year and told me he not only knew about the S-ANTA, but also that I must have killed his father. He was quite upset, but thanks to his little fairy's soft heart I was given the time I needed to plan my counter-attack."

"She believed in second chances," Kertas said through gritted teeth.

"Isn't that precious? Too bad it meant she had to die, as well."

"You're a monster," Kertas growled.

I put a branch out to stop him from throttling the cookie. "We both know the truth now. Nick knows, too. Nick always knows."

"Of course he does. 'He knows when you've been bad or good.' Too bad he didn't figure it out till it was too late to save three people." Merry took a step back. "As I said, my work here is done. There's no stopping what I've already put in motion. There's really only one thing left to do."

"No, wait!" I cried, but it was too late.

With a giant leap, the cookie threw himself backward into the lake, the cold, white surface swallowing him up in one gulp.

Kertas and I stood at the milky edge and removed our hats, holding them over our hearts.

"God rest ye, Merry Gingerbread Man."

Epilogue

"Victor, his name is Victor," Fragile told me as we approached the squirrel tapping away on the S-ANTA computer.

Luckily, it turned out her husband had a knack for IT.

"So can you fix it?" I asked.

"Indubitably," he said, scratching his chin. "It's a good thing you were able to tell me exactly what I'd be looking for, otherwise I might have gotten lost in all of this. It's unlike any code I've ever seen."

"Too bad the programmer went nuts," muttered Kertas. "So you'll take the job?" he asked Victor.

"Yes, sir, count me in. It would be an honor to be the one who not only fixed the S-ANTA, but kept it up and running for many Christmases to come."

Kertas shook the squirrel's hand and turned to me. "It's a good thing you found this guy. I don't know what we would have done. We might have had to go back to the old way of doing things."

"Heaven forbid," I said with a smile. "Seems to me the old way worked a few hundred years longer than the new way."

On Christmas morning, I was gifted a new scarf, handmade by Kertas.

"I didn't know you knitted."

"It's crochet, but I have to admit, my mom whipped it together for me. Figured it would be nice for you to have something to remember me by for next year. You will remember me next year, won't you?" he asked.

It warmed my heart to see him so worried. "How could I ever forget you?" Especially since I'd made certain his name and our memories of the past few days filled my notebook this time. It was getting so full, I'd need a new one soon enough.

"Merry Christmas," I said, handing him my gift.

"Aw, Shovel, you shouldn't have," he said, then pulled out the box of two hundred candles.

His face split into what might have been the first real, full smile I'd seen cross his face since we'd met.

"Think those'll last you a couple weeks?" I asked.

"Couple days more like, but I'll try to make them last that long."

"You know what they say: No snowman is a failure who has friends."

"Aw, shucks."

"It was the least I could do. Thank you for helping me, Kertas."

"Anytime, Shovel, anytime."

Kertas's eyes focused on the candle in his hand. "All I wanted for Christmas was you," he murmured softly. Then he took a big bite out of it and grinned.

The rest of my time passed in a lovely, glorious, beautiful Christmas blur.

Before I knew it, I'd come to the end. I was surrounded by friends new and old: Kertas, Nick, Nora, Mrs. Cane, Dr. Flick, Fragile, Victor, even Snegurka with whom I'd enjoyed a sleigh ride or two, as well as a kiss under the mistletoe.

"It's gonna be boring without you," said Kertas. "What am I supposed to do all year without you around?"

"I don't know," I shrugged. "Run a business? Steal some candles? Practice your song lyrics?"

Kertas smiled and wrapped his gifted scarf around my neck.

"You really brought home the spirit of Christmas this year, to all of us," he said. "Perhaps that's your true purpose?"

"What? To solve murders?"

"Perhaps you *are* the Spirit of Christmas."

As I began to slowly melt away, I saw Kertas put a comforting arm around Nick Claus's shoulder, his voice piercing through the fog. "Don't worry, he'll be back again someday."

THE END

Recipes

BABA NOËL'S EGYPTIAN KAHK

Kahk Dough:

1 T yeast
1 T sugar
⅓ C warm milk
1 ¼ C butter
3 C flour (all-purpose)
½ tsp cinnamon

Agameya Filling:

3 T butter
2 T flour
1 C honey
1 C pistachios (or walnuts)
2 tsp sesame seeds

Directions:

1. Dissolve the sugar and yeast in the warm milk and set to the side.
2. Melt the butter until it's bubbling.
3. In a heat-resistant bowl, mix the flour and cinnamon. Make a well in the center and pour in the melted butter. Stir with a spoon until completely mixed. Leave to cool.
4. Once the flour mixture has cooled down—about 10-15 minutes—check it with your fingers to be sure it is all combined. Add the milk mixture and mix until it becomes a dough. Let sit for one hour.
5. While the dough sits, prepare the agameya filling. Melt the butter in a pan on the stovetop.
6. Whisk the flour in the pan once the butter is melted to make a roux.
7. Remove it from the heat to add the honey, pistachios, and sesame seeds.
8. Put the mixture back onto the heat at a low temperature, stirring until it thickens, then back off the heat to cool until you can form it into small balls—the smaller the better.
9. Once the dough has finished resting for that hour, preheat oven to 350°F (175°C).
10. Take a piece of dough and flatten it until it will just cover one of the agameya balls. Place one of the balls in the center of the dough and wrap the dough around it. Roll it against your palm until you have a nice, smooth ball. Collect them on a baking sheet.

11. Now comes the fun part: the design. You can purchase a wooden mold specifically designed for *kahk* which makes a beautiful carving on the surface. OR try pressing the ball into other molds you have to make unique designs. OR using a fork, press a simple design across the surface. Get creative with it!
12. Bake at 350°F (175°C) for 15 minutes or until golden brown.
13. Coat with powdered sugar once cool. Store in an airtight container to enjoy at your next Christmas party!

MERRY'S GINGERBREAD COOKIES (BEFORE CARROT ADDITION!)

Ingredients:

3 ¼ C flour (all-purpose)
¾ tsp baking soda
½ tsp salt
½ tsp cloves
½ tsp nutmeg
1 T ginger
1 T cinnamon
¼ tsp pepper (more if you like them spicy)
¾ C butter, softened
½ C brown sugar
1 egg
½ C molasses

Directions:

1. Whisk together the flour, baking soda, and spices.
2. In an electric mixer, beat the butter and brown sugar until light and fluffy, about 2 minutes.
3. Add the eggs and molasses and beat until combined.
4. Mix in the flour mixture a little at a time. You should end up with a stiff dough.
5. Chill in the refrigerator at least 1 hour.
6. Once the dough has chilled long enough, remove it from the refrigerator and let it come to room temperature while you preheat the oven to 350°F (175°C).
7. On a floured surface, roll out the dough in sections with a floured rolling pin. Cut into your favorite Christmas cookie cutter shapes! (If you roll it thick, you'll end up with chewier cookies.)
8. Bake at 350°F (175°C) for 8-10 minutes.
9. Let cool and store in an airtight container or freeze for a Christmas cookie decorating party!

Acknowledgements

Merry Christmas, everyone!

I pray this book was as much fun to read as it was to write!

"For God so loved the world that He gave His only Son that whoever believes in Him shall not die but have eternal life." This Christmas, I am reminded of why the themes of love, joy, and unity seem so prevalent at this time of year. I am eternally grateful to my Lord and Savior, who sent His Son to live and die for me, and continues to give me the words to write!

Special thanks to my husband, to whom I am especially grateful since he had to look up pronunciations for all the non-English words in this book for the audiobook!

To my children, who I pray will never lose the joy and wonder of Christmastime.

To my parents, for ensuring I grew up with a magical Christmas full of Christmas cookies, Christmas movies (but only after Thanksgiving!), and Christmas carols galore!

To my parents-in-law, for establishing Christmas cookie decorating day as one of my kids' favorite traditions.

To my editor, Corin Faye, who said this was one of his favorite Christmas books ever written and is already requesting a sequel and a movie.

My amazing team of Beta Readers: Noelle Austin, Kathy Buckmaster, Corin Faye, Anne Fischer, Diane Gordon, Brenda McCosby, Maggie Meredith, Renae Meredith, Scotte Meredith, Lydia Pierce, Sue Rizzo, and Rebecca Writz.

And you, dear Reader. Thank you for taking the time to read this book! Would you please leave me a review so I know how much you loved it?

If you'd like to learn more about all the Christmas traditions, references, and food sprinkled throughout this book, be sure to visit my website at Patricia-Meredith.com, my YouTube channel @pmeredithauthor, and follow me on social media as @pmeredithauthor.

Thank you for reading and merry Christmas!

Patricia Meredith traveled all the way to the North Pole and around the world to ensure this story was the most accurate representation of true events not previously shared outside of the Santa Network. As an author of cozy mysteries, she took time out of her day to test delicious recipes, learn the finer points of moon-bathing, master how to beat a reindeer at a card game, and interview the current North Pole Santa Claus.

For all the latest updates, you can follow her as @pmeredithauthor on YouTube, Goodreads, Instagram, and Facebook, and sign up for her newsletter at Patricia-Meredith.com.

www.ingramcontent.com/pod-product-compliance
Lightning Source LLC
Chambersburg PA
CBHW020329030826
48979CB00021B/500

* 9 7 8 1 0 8 8 0 4 1 9 0 1 *